One Hundred Thousand Lives After Death

Megan Lee Bees

ELENRY PRESS

This is a work of fiction. All of the characters, organizations, and events portrayed in this novella are either products of the author's imagination, or are used fictitiously.

ONE HUNDRED THOUSAND LIVES AFTER DEATH

An Elenry Press Book

Copyright © 2026 by Megan Lee Bees

All Rights Reserved

No part of this book may be reproduced or transmitted in any form without permission from the author, except as permitted by U.S. copyright law.

For permissions contact: meganleebees@protonmail.com

ISBN:

Cover image © by Megan Lee Bees

Cover and book design by Megan Lee Bees

For Erik

Content Warning:

This is a book of horror.

While there is a love story at its core, there is also broken bones, claustrophobia, a grotesque depiction of animal death, an allusion to pet death, murder, child endangerment, a brief mention of suicide, and at least one-hundred-thousand spiders.

If this is something you are not looking for in a story, than I thank you for your interest thus far, and I hope to catch you on the next one. If all of this sounds fine for you, then take my hand. I promise it will all work out in the end.

Especially if you have a fondness for monsters.

The Wife, Tillie Wright, was in the garden. Her many fangs chewed through stems that would taste grassy and bright if she still had a living tongue. Flowers dropped neatly down to her hundreds of outstretched and waiting claws. It was a joyful task, on a brilliant spring afternoon, and she marched her bouquet happily through the open kitchen door on the procession of spiders that carried her soul as easily as they carried flowers.

The Artist, Tillie Wright, was at a retreat one hundred and twenty seven miles away, with the effervescent Newberry Award Nominee E. Leilani Liu. She sketched alongside her, sitting in companionable silence at the shore of the Columbia River as one thousand miniscule spiders operated her hand with ease. The bones she designed and printed in resin made her disguise perfect, and so long as she stayed out of the water, no one at the retreat would ever guess that the human Tillie Wright had been dead for over ten years.

The Hunger, which had no name, was in the forest. It was building bodies, many bodies, some occupied, most not. No matter where else Tillie was, The Hunger was always hungry, and it was always in the forest.

Part One
The Wife

The spiders that made The Wife swarmed up within the body she kept in the closet. They filled their stations and animated the thing to near-life as a horde of them carried her out of the closet door to greet Ivan at the bottom of the stairs.

Ivan still had his headset on when Tillie surrounded his desk in a carpet of flowers. He looked away from his computer screen and swept his eyes over the floor, then the room, until he found one of the older spiders lounging on a shelf between a few dusty workplace awards. None of the spiders could claim to be any more Tillie than the rest, but Ivan preferred to address the elders when he could. They were big enough to afford him some eye contact. He would never admit it aloud, but he sometimes missed the days when she only had two eyes, when he didn't have to choose which of her thousands to focus on.

"Noon already?" he asked.

The spider stood and bobbed its head up and down, and then scuttled down the wall to join the carpet of flowers that was flowing out of the room and down the stairs.

He smiled and set his headset back on just long enough to finish off his meeting with a round of pleasantries.

Downstairs, Tillie had misjudged the capacity of her vase by a wide margin. She ferried some of the lesser used mugs out on strands of spidersilk and cut the excess flowers into multiple miniature bouquets, but there were still too many flowers. Perhaps she'd make wreaths for every door in the house.

The floor creaked overhead with Ivan's footsteps and she gathered her body from its space in the closet, the bones of the woman who died ten years ago.

She and Ivan had perfected some things in the time since her spiders had devoured the last of her flesh. They'd fitted the skull with a silicone tongue and soft palate which allowed her to mimic the voice that died with the body. She'd packed dense cobweb beneath her silken skin to give Ivan something soft to hold. A mask, a perfect mimicry of the face she'd once had, with fine-tuned lifts and pulleys embedded within, allowed a team of spiders to make expressions at a pace which only lagged imperceptibly behind the emotions she felt. It was so near to being human that she hardly even missed it anymore.

Although, she never did manage to get the hang of the legs. She'd placed those in a box and tucked them away in the attic on the bottom of a dusty bookshelf. Boxes of model trains were stacked on top, and the legs were only acknowledged when she and Ivan needed to change his diorama from passenger cars to freight. Any thought for the legs passed quickly as the trains were tucked into their boxes.

Her hands were always working, even when the body was at rest. She kept them in the studio, disembodied puppets that could paint whatever came to mind for the team that controlled them. At the moment, they were keyed to The Artist one hundred and twenty-seven miles away, and they copied the movement of her plastic hands with such precision that the paper they painted would have been an exact replica of hers, if only the studio's greens would behave. The Artist had the benefit of new paints, but the hands in her studio were making do with old and overmixed.

The spiders that made The Wife swarmed up within the body she kept in the closet. They filled their stations and animated the thing to near-life as a horde of them carried her out of the closet door to greet Ivan at the bottom of the stairs.

"Are those zinnias?" he asked of the mug of flowers trundling up the stairs on the backs of multiple spiders. He rubbed his eyes and patted his pockets. His computer readers were pushing back his thinning hair, and a spider raced down the banister with his day glasses held up to meet his hand. He adjusted them over his nose with a murmured thank you as another spider swept the readers from his head and scuttled off to set them back in their case.

She pressed a laugh through the painted lips and shook the skull, no. The zinnias wouldn't be in bloom for months. Spiders worked the bellows of her woven lungs, pressed silicon tongue to teeth, and started up her voice. "Daisies, mostly. A couple crocus, and a few sprigs of onion." Ivan thought any flower that wasn't a rose might be a zinnia.

Ivan took her delicate shoulders, drew her near, and kissed the mask's cheek. "Onion! We'll have bouquets for dinner!" He laughed as she pulled a face. "I don't have any more tickets lined up today. Why don't I take the afternoon off and we put on a movie?"

"Are you sure they don't need you?" she asked. Ivan had some kind of consulting job with computers, and though he often spoke of his work, his clients and capabilities were as mysterious to her as the magic that kept her consciousness alive.

He shook his head. "I thought we could have some time together. Something low-impact. I know you're at the retreat right now, too."

She nodded. Tillie had lost count of how many minds belonged to her after reaching one hundred thousand spiders. It was far too many for a single consciousness to hold them, and so she turned her focus to art, to living, and to life with her sweet husband. The house spiders lived with Ivan, the hands handled painting, the plastic body handled friends.

The rest were unthinkable, unmanageable, and so she did not think of them, and let them manage themselves.

"Whatever you want, honey," she answered. "A movie sounds nice."

※ ※ ※

On the shore of the Columbia River, where it opens its mouth wide to the yawning Pacific, and its waters mix with salt, E. Leilani Liu asked The Artist Tillie Wright if she'd want to do this again.

This: Twelve close friends who'd never met in person before last week. Each of them artists: five watercolorists, three ink, two gouache, two charcoal. A small collection of cabins overlooking the water, resources pooled and distributed to accommodate everyone's needs. A chance to grow in one's art and forget the troubles of home for a week.

"We haven't even finished the first one," Tillie answered with a cheeky smile. Her hands were painting the waves lapping against the shore as lovingly as she could manage, but it was hard to feel much affection for something that would destroy her body and drown her spiders if she happened to fall in. Still, the book she was meant to illustrate was set on the ocean, and she wanted to do right by the waves. She could never get the picture right until she found something to love in it.

E. Leilani Liu laughed at the dumb little joke and Tillie smiled wide because she loved to hear the woman laugh and because Tillie and Ivan had spent so much time perfecting her teeth that it would be a shame not to smile. The first batch had been inhumanly white when Ivan printed them in plastic, and they'd melted a little in the afternoon sun when Tillie forgot to move them from the window. It took three rounds with the printer to get the color right, and another ten to find the balance of fleshy red gums to set them in.

She wished she could show Leilani the lovely opalescent shade of pearl-pink she'd chosen for her skull, but it was impossible to bring up the color of one's bones without admitting the soft mask of one's face covered a multitude of spiders. And so she turned back toward her painting and daubed some white in where light would show through the green water.

Terrible. It looked even worse than before. Maybe she was not meant to love the ocean.

Leilani coughed next to her, reminding Tillie they'd been talking.

"You're always good with the newer artists online, do you want to take on an instructor role if we made this a formal event next year?"

"Oh!"

Leaving the house at all was so difficult. The retreat took almost a year of planning. But E. Leilani Liu was such a gracious host, friendly and accommodating. Tillie was not the only artist in their group who used a wheelchair, and Leilani herself sometimes used a cane.

Although the cabins were small and oddly shaped, rising from the mossy ground like cedarwood origami, the paths were paved, and the ramps were well built. A wheelchair was ideal for Tillie's disguise, but she still worried she might slip.

Ten years of playing human, and the spiders had still never managed to work the legs. It was easy for her to move outside of the body, to split herself into a swarm and carry whatever piece of her soul wished to go, wherever it wished to be. And while it would be a simple task to swarm and carry her hands down to the edge of the surf where they could make portraits of the little rock crabs that waved at her from afar, it would surely terrify her friends. Being able to split one's whims between swarms of spiders and carry out all of them simultaneously made a lot of things easy, but it did make finding friends exceptionally difficult.

Tillie had to relearn friendship after she died. The illness that had killed her worked slowly. It first stripped her down to a husk, and as it stole from her life, her world became small. Friends fell away as the places she once belonged to became out of reach, until it was only Ivan and herself. Ivan and herself and Ivan's broken heart, because he knew she would leave him behind.

But Tillie survived had her death. It was not a pretty survival. She'd hidden it as best she could, but Ivan had found out eventually. And, in a miracle that she still did not understand, he hadn't run away. He'd listened and he'd stayed. And when they got a bit of money, him with a better job and her with more and more commissions, they'd both moved out of the city to a little house on the edge of a wild forest, where she did not have to hide away inside their home. Where she could abscond to the forest and feel the sun again.

It was Tillie's sister who allowed her to survive her own death. Mavis was a witch. She did what she could. But Mavis left as soon as she'd solved the problem of death, and she never returned.

Tillie got on. She sold illustrations. She practiced friendship on artist forums. She got invited to smaller chatrooms, which turned into private talks late at night with friends across the world. Eventually, they started to talk of meeting up, and Tillie had spoken to Ivan about the logistics of creating a better body that would allow her to live again amongst the living.

It was lonely still, to be without family, but her sister had been gone for so long that the ache was familiar. A hole where a tooth should be, where the tongue would come to rest. She could live with that ache.

When spread across a hundred thousand bodies, she could hardly feel the ache at all.

* * *

The Wife turned to Ivan with a wide grin as she relayed The Artist's conversation: "She's asking if I want to be an instructor next year!"

Ivan brightened and raised his hands in victory.

Tillie squirmed with joy. "I think I have a professional crush."

He laughed. "On E. Leilani Liu? You sing her whole name every time she's mentioned."

Tillie wheezed a little laugh through the papery lungs and knocked her shoulder against his. "She does the prettiest fluffiest moths in charcoals. And they're so expressive! She still has some originals from her first book and I'm buying one the moment my check from that magazine clears."

"Maybe we could hang it in the kitchen," said Ivan. His hand stroked absently, fondly, across one of her oldest spiders. It was as large as a baseball, fuzzed over like a kiwi, with legs as thick as Ivan's fingers.

Her mind briefly went into it, and she pushed herself into his hand, scraped her fangs softly against the pad of his thumb, and the affection spread out through her network of spiders like honey on hot toast, golden and sweet.

"Were I the moth eating type," he mused, "I think Ms. Liu's would look pretty appetizing."

Tillie pulled the mask of her face into an exaggerated grimace and stuck out her tongue. "They're so dry, honey. They're better as caterpillars."

He hummed thoughtfully and went to the kitchen. "Do we have caterpillars in the shed right now or just crickets?" he asked.

"Just crickets." The nursery shed in the backyard was filled with boxes of them, separated by age so the adults wouldn't gobble up all the tasty little grubs that couldn't run or fight. She needed to rotate them soon, or the eggs that had sifted down through the mesh would hatch outside her boxes. It was little trouble to catch larvae. They were slow and deliciously easy to devour, but then she'd have to start over with breading insects, she didn't want to waste another thousand dollars while she was also saving up for a fluffy moth in charcoal.

And it wouldn't do to go hungry. She was always so hungry. She'd lost track of how many mouths she had to feed. There were no naturally occurring insects nearby anymore. Nor birds, or rats or squirrels or deer...

"Why, are you hungry?" she asked, when she remembered he was standing in the kitchen, waiting for an answer. She kept dropping conversations while her mind was in the forest, at the sea, in the studio, and everywhere else. She had to focus. Here. With him. "I could eat."

"I'm making popcorn, and we're watching a movie. I could dust it with cricket flour if you're interested."

"I'll share some popcorn," she said, pulling the mask over her polished skull into a pleasant smile.

He frowned slightly, like she'd done something wrong. "Your hands are missing."

Her hands were in the studio, suspended in silk, disembodied and unbothered by the weight of humanity as they echoed the movement of her brushstrokes a hundred miles away. "They're painting."

Ivan sighed, disappointed. "You have a whole other body that's already painting at the coast. You're spread too thin! If you need to go dormant here so you can focus there, please. Go." He blew a kiss to the body on the couch, then scritched the head of a spider on the counter. "I mean, I love having you, but you should be with your friends."

"It's fine! The hands are just copying what the retreat body is doing. It's barely a thought."

He shook his head and put the popcorn back on the shelf. "No movie, then. Go! Paint your oceans!"

"I'm fine, Ivan! When you don't have to worry about operating legs—"

"Sweetheart, I do not think about my legs that much. Nobody thinks about their legs as much as you think they do."

"Yes, but your body works all over, without you having to think about it—"

He suddenly looked so sad, and Tillie dropped the fight.

The problem with storing one's soul in a multitude of spiders is that the soul can very quickly outgrow them. Spiders are small; their little minds can only carry so much. Each day, each experience needed a place to go, and when Tillie ran into the ceiling of her many minds' capacity, she found it was little trouble to create more of them.

So she did.

She laid eggs, she hatched, and she had space again for more memory, more soul, more and more and more. And Ivan thought it was wonderful that she never forgot a thing, that she had perfect recall on every moment of her life from the moment she returned from the dead.

And if he was a little sad when she could not recall something from before, some moment when she was still human—a first date at a soda fountain, a hat she'd made with snowflakes knit around the band—he was very good at hiding it. If her eyes hadn't numbered in the thousands, if they were not always watching from countless angles, attuned to the tiniest quake of movement, she would not have seen his sorrow.

He didn't speak of it. And neither did she. And they were happy, because every happy person is a little sad sometimes.

"I'll fetch my hands." The strands holding them snapped as quickly as thought. They marched into the kitchen and waved their fingers at him until his face lifted a little, then neatly climbed her body to reattach at the wrists.

"There!" She waggled the hands to test their hold, then twisted them around to frame her face and make goggles of her fingers. "Now we can watch a movie." She grinned.

He nodded with pursed lips, unamused by her antics. "You worry me sometimes."

She dropped her hands away and pulled him close. "You don't need to worry about me," she whispered, and squeezed her hand around his arm. She never wanted him to worry about her.

She was not an easy creature to love. All her bodies, all her hungry mouths, all her wretched little thoughts that she banished to the forest when she could not bear to keep them in the house.

He didn't need to know about The Hunger.

And she did not need to think of it.

She thought of her friends at the river, her painting hands, her perfect husband, all while the claws in the forest were building and building and building and she was watching a movie on the couch.

Something animated, well past the opening scene.

How long have they been watching this movie?

"I'm fine, Ivan. I promise."

He looked at her oddly. He hadn't said anything to provoke that response. Who was she responding to?

The doorbell chimed. He kissed her head. He went to answer the door, and Tillie was alone.

❦ ❦ ❦

"You don't have to answer right away. You got a year to think on it."

Tillie remembered suddenly that E. Leilani Liu was watching her patiently. Her hands were moving without thought, the spiders that worked beneath her silken skin pulling the strands inside her fingers to move her paintbrush neatly across the page.

"I couldn't commit to anything yet," she said. The smile she wore did not match her thoughts. She wanted to say yes. She had gone a decade without being seen by anyone but Ivan, and she was unwilling to give that up. People liked her here. People were kind. "I want to."

Leilani reached out to her, and Tillie forced herself to be still, to not draw away. Leilani took her hand, woven tendons and plastic bones beneath the soft silk skin. And yes, it was magic that kept the woman from knowing the horrors that animated Tillie's body. Her sister's spellwork kept Tillie spinning in this facsimile of life, but it was more than that. It was a miracle: a miracle that she could be touched and still cared for.

"Then we'll make it happen," said E. Leilani Liu. Her lovely dark eyes crinkled at that, and she patted Tillie on the shoulder. "You should get inside soon, though. Your hands are freezing!"

She should get inside. She should focus here, on this place, in the body she'd built for it, and not on a distant doorbell ringing. Still ringing. Ringing frantically, even though it hardly ever rang. There shouldn't be any company until Sunday.

"Is it lunch already?" asked Tillie. Lunch was inside. She had been eating privately in her cabin while the others cavorted in the dining hall. She tried to eat quickly, swarming out of the skin to devour what was offered. Yesterday was a lovely falafel. Good texture. She wished she could have commented on it to her friends, but it was long past time for that when she rejoined them, and besides, she couldn't have them asking her to join them for their next meal. She didn't want to keep saying no to the things she wanted.

"Lunch isn't until one. Are you still eating in your cabin?"

"Always." Tillie forced a light chuckle. "Maybe I am a touch off. I think I need to lie down. Can I leave my paper here?"

"Of course," said Leilani.

Tillie closed her paintbox and slipped it into the case she mounted on the back of her chair. In her haste to leave, she left a paintbrush laying on her paper. It rolled down the page and dotted her skirt with green before clattering to the ground, thankfully missing Leilani's canvas by an inch.

Tillie didn't think to apologize until she was nearly to her cabin. She gripped her wheels, slowed from the frantic pace she'd taken and pressed a practiced breath through her silken lungs.

She was losing focus. She was elsewhere. She was frightened.

Why was she frightened?

🕷 🕷 🕷

There were no animals in the forest within a mile of Tillie's house. The Hunger was the only thing that lived there, and it was forever expanding its range.

A calculating force, an endless and devouring mass: the countless horde of spiders worked with a singular mind, and it required food. The bugs were gone. Their work of decomposition was abandoned. The birds no longer sang. Raccoons and deer and rabbits made their dens far from the little gray house with the bright yellow shutters and the thing that surrounded it.

Tillie had lied to Ivan. She kept lying, with every moment she lived inside his house, letting him think that there were only two bodies which the spiders operated. She had presented her design for the plastic model as a lark, as if it only came to her because of the invitation to an artist's retreat, when she couldn't bear to let her precious bones leave his sight.

She had known that the body crafted for the retreat would work, because The Hunger had already built so many others.

When it was not eating, it was fulfilling the duties of the creatures it devoured. Spiders chittered in reconstructed birds. Spiders chewed dead wood and scattered seeds and churned the soil as they hunted for worms to devour. The Hunger built the forest to suit itself, and made a home out of its exile.

The thing that The Hunger wore when it walked together through its wooded realm had a hundred arms and innumerable rib cages lashed together, buttressed with antlers and other bone to make a frame for its body. It had no face. A crown made from a hundred broken jaws was affixed to the front of the thing, stripped of its flesh. Its polished teeth glittered like jewels.

Within the deep forest, light and shame could not touch The Hunger. It could desire to hunt and kill and keep that desire away from Tillie's perfect and human husband and all his civilized ways. It could track a herd of elk, single out the largest among the massive beasts, and all its fangs could salivate at the thought of its death.

Today, The Hunger left its body far from the herd while its spiders crawled silently toward the elk. It would eat well, then dry the bones and add them to its body when all the flesh was picked clean.

The Hunger chose its mark, a larger buck standing sentry out from the pack, waiting to alert his fellows to any danger.

The elk flicked his tail as a strand of silk landed over his haunches. Another drifted across his neck. He stilled, snorted, and looked around for the hunter, but he did not see the carpet of spiders weaving around his legs. He bolted, and ropes of spidersilk cinched around his hooves. He fell hard to the ground and bellowed in fear at the sharp rock that pierced his side. He kicked, again and again, but the spiders rushed over his body and clung easily to his fur. A few of the larger spiders punctured his eyes as he thrashed, allowing the smaller ones to enter through the gore. Still more crowded into his ears, pressing through the wax until they found an entrance to the skull.

It was dark inside the skull. The disorienting slosh of a struggling beast made finding the spinal cord difficult. The cerebral fluid might drown half the tiny spiders that make it into the brain, but The Hunger had birthed these spiders for this purpose. They were tethered to the collective consciousness, but had no memory of their own. Empty of soul, they were allowed to die.

The elk slowed its thrashing as the spinal cord began to fray.

The Hunger's body approached. Its first four arms raised high, and with fingertips made of wolves' teeth, it pierced the body of the elk and killed it.

The Hunger crashed over the fallen elk and drug its heavy claws through the hide, splitting open the hot flesh to allow for an easier meal. The spiders descended on it. They ate. The fang sharp hands split the skull and exposed steaming brain and drowned spiders, and The Hunger ate them too.

The Hunger thought rarely of the body inside the house, of the Tillie that lived with her husband, but there was always a tether. Always some soft sound of domesticity ringing in the distance of its mind. It was ringing louder today. Again and again. Like a doorbell.

How odd.

The Hunger had little understanding of time, but it was almost certain that The Wife was not expecting visitors.

※ ※ ※

Ivan was answering the door. Tillie could not remember when he'd left her side, if he'd spoken to her, if she heard the doorbell or a knock. The front door was far from the den, where a movie was flashing colors across the rainbow blanket he'd left her in, across the dark blue velvet couch, across the glittering pinpricks of her thousands of eyes. Something important was happening on the screen, if the swell of the music was to be believed, but she still didn't know what movie was playing.

She pulled her body up from the couch. She should check her appearance, see if she was suitable for guests. Her face was a little ragged, her wrists threadbare. Was it the second Sunday already? When the neighbor woman left her daughter for the afternoon so she could pick up another shift at the hospital?

A small team of spiders worked to reinforce her tendons as her focus shifted into the eyes of a spider crouched inside the whorls of the crown molding in the entryway. It was not the neighbors at the door. Ivan would not greet Surena and Ava so rigidly, with his knuckles white where he gripped the doorknob. She dropped down on a thread, and saw her sister standing there.

She had not seen Mavis in a decade.

Her hair was shorn close. Her clothes were rumpled and pilled. Her eyes were bruised and hollow and she carried a small bird caged in her fingers. Ivan called for Tillie, said something to Mavis, tried to make pleasantries— he was always afraid of Mavis.

Tillie understood his fear.

"I need to speak to her," said Mavis, and she stomped past him with the bird clutched to her chest. She navigated the house like it was her own and found Tillie's body hiding in the den.

Tillie's mind fled. She could only hear the ocean crashing against cold rocks. The bones in the forest. The scuttling of her countless feet, swarming away from Mavis to hide her hideous shapes in the darkest corners of her cheery little home.

"Hello Creature," said Mavis.

Tillie's consciousness crashed into the body in the den, and all her spiders swarmed to their sentries, plucked their strands tight, and pulled the puppet of herself to attention.

Creature was not inaccurate. But it did sting that Mavis chose "creature" first. Above "sister," above "Tillie," or any of the silly little pet names she used to call her when she was little and Mavis was the elder sister with all the answers in the world.

Tillie took the hurt, rolled it into a tight little ball, and gave it to one of the smaller spiders to carry off into the woods. If Mavis noticed the hurt spider fleeing the room, she did not mention it. Nor did Ivan.

It was silly to think that any would notice a single spider out of the hundred thousand that made her. She was being silly, to assume sympathy for a pain she did not air.

"Why are you here, Mavis?" asked Ivan. His jaw was set. His voice shook, but he was resilient.

Ivan never ran, no matter how afraid. He was incredible. Tillie was always running. There was always some cowardly piece of her that fled for the forest, and if she didn't have so many bodies, Ivan might have noticed by now how terribly fearful his wife had become. Ivan only had one body, but he always kept it steadily beside her, even as it trembled.

Mavis did not acknowledge him, or his bravery. Her eyes bore into the empty sockets of Tillie's skull.

The bird screeched horribly and pecked against Mavis's hands. Each finger was bandaged, and every bandage looked old. Her hands were flecked over with tiny scars, white against ashen skin. She looked as if she hadn't seen the sun since she left ten years ago.

"I need your help. I don't have anywhere else to go." Mavis had never spoken an apology before. She never spoke with anything less than the highest authority, and even now, rumpled and ragged and caging a wild bird in her hands, she still spoke to Tillie like a parent. "But I won't pretend that you're my sister."

Something broke. Miles away, in a little cabin near the place where the river met the sea, a body fell to pieces. Deep inside the forest, a clatter of bones hit the wet earth. A wave of hurt buffeted her, and spiders dropped away from her body to carry that hurt away before it could fester in her heart.

"I'm all that's left of her, Mavis. And I still love you."

She had been so careful with her feelings around Mavis. She plucked away every thought of hurt or sadness and sent it all into the forest where The Hunger could lock it away, and all Tillie had for her was love. It was gossamer thin, more holes than not, but it was love.

"We sent you Christmas cards," said Ivan, the venom in his tone like an accusation.

She'd been the only one on the list. But the cards were returned without a forwarding address, and phone calls went unanswered. Mavis had dropped off the face of the earth. Tillie stopped trying.

And with time, she stopped living in that loneliness.

She had friends now. She was capable and good and she didn't have to be Mavis's monstrous little sister. She had her masks and her paints and a community that saw the artist and not the spiders, that never knew what lurked beneath her skin. And when she sent cards to those friends, she got cards back.

Tillie smiled. All her hurt and hate and sadness was fleeing for the forest where she did not have to see it. She was better. She made her voice pretty and pulled the blanket further around herself and asked so kindly, "Why are you holding that bird?"

Mavis's thin lips drew to an even tighter line. She looked as though her whole head could crack apart at the seam of her lips and the skull would slide off her jaw and shatter against the floor. "He's my son."

The bird peeped and fluttered and banged against her fingers. She brought it to her face, kissed the cage of knuckles and whispered to him. "It's okay, Freddie. She's not going to hurt you."

Mavis looked down at Tillie; at the skeletal figure draped in a blanket, the bones strung together and padded with cobweb. The empty eye sockets and the undulating mass of spiders that swarmed beneath it. Tillie cursed herself for leaving her glass eyes in their plastic box on the bedside table. She didn't think she'd need them for a movie day.

"You won't hurt him," said Mavis, with steel in her eyes and her mouth set. "You have to help us."

Tillie took another blanket from the back of the couch, the pretty woven one showing various mushrooms and their taxonomy, and draped it over her shoulders to further hide her body. She wished she had the mask she'd sent to E. Leilani Liu's retreat. She wished she could breathe, but panic was shimmering across the spiders, making even the false working of her lungs difficult. More of them tumbled down the blankets and ran for the forest. They rushed out of the room in droves to carry her panic away. Couldn't they see her moving across the floor? How could they not see the way she was losing herself?

"You have a son?" she asked, because it was important. Mavis had a son. She was an aunt, even if Mavis had never told her of him, and that seemed like an important thing to suddenly be.

She should look like an aunt. She reached through her connection to ask a spider to bring her eyes downstairs, but she couldn't feel any but the spiders nearby.

"He's cursed," said Mavis. "I can't help him."

Tillie barked a stupid laugh and Mavis glared at her. "What would I know about curses?"

Mavis's eyes swept over the room. The den was dark, but it opened to a sunroom. With all its leafy potted plants and spiders lurking in the dirt, bodies pressed against cool earth and watching with all their eyes. She chewed her lip. Her brows furrowed in anger. "I don't know anyone else with magic." Her mouth twitched like she was swallowing ash.

Tillie shook her head. Mavis was the one with magic. Tillie was strung together with it, but she didn't understand it any better than she knew Ivan's computers.

The little bird pounded against Mavis's hand, shrieking in terror. Tillie could feel the drive to hunt shiver across her backs. She'd eaten so many birds just like him over the years. She knew the taste of that terror.

More of her left the horde, carrying her hunger away. The remaining spiders dug their claws into her bones and wrenched themselves into humanity as she smiled and softened her face and spoke with so much care and sorrow, "I'm not a witch, Mavis."

Ivan stepped up, and placed himself slightly in front of Tillie. In front of the bones, the skull, and the mass of spiders that operated her, but Tillie still surrounded them. She was in the houseplants and corners of rooms and underfoot, swarming out the door.

"Why don't you explain this curse," said Ivan.

She spoke past him. "It's a punishment for what I did to you. It has to be—"

"Mavis, you saved my life. That's what you did to me." Tillie reached for her, because it didn't matter that her bodies were in panic or that she was subtly fleeing for the door. She was made of love, and she loved her sister still, no matter how much it hurt. She said it again. "I love you."

"You don't. You're just a ghost of her."

Of course she was a ghost. But she was still herself, in the way that mattered.

"Stop," said Ivan. "I want to be able to say we're glad to see you, Mavis, but not like this. You vanish for ten years, and then show up to call my wife a monster. I think you need to start with an apology."

"Your wife?" Mavis shook her head. "How is the spell still holding?" she muttered. "How do you not see what she is?" She shifted to look at him, and as she did, her fingers opened ever so slightly. She yelped. Tiny claws tore red ribbons into her skin, and the bird shot out of her hands. Mavis fell after it, clawing at the empty air. It fluttered high and tore through cobwebs hiding in the ceiling fan, then darted for the windows in the sun room.

"Catch him!" shouted Mavis.

Tillie swarmed out from the corners of the room. All the hundreds of her that had stayed inside the house while the rest of her was fleeing for the forest. She couldn't climb fast enough. She didn't have enough bodies to corner him. Freddie bobbed at the glass and smacked his little head against it until he bounced upward to the little window she'd opened that morning to let in the fresh spring air. He clambered through it. He fell out, a looping ball of feathers, then opened his wings and caught himself, arcing upward toward the forest, wings pumping furiously to draw him along. In moments he was already difficult to see.

Something horrible and guttural tore out of Mavis's throat. Something like *no*, like *stop*, like all the sorrow in the world made manifest.

Her hand reached helplessly for the escaping bird.

He was gone.

Mavis turned on Tillie.

A spilled popcorn bowl lay between them. It was heavy, stoneware, something picked up from a thrift store ages ago that looked built to last hundreds of years. Mavis hefted it up, popcorn flew from it and scattered around her, and she threw it at Tillie's skeleton. Her ribs crunched inward as she collapsed around its impact.

Ivan flew at Mavis and wrestled her arms down, but she fell and pulled them both to the ground, kicking at every spider she could see, squashing them and breaking legs.

Tillie had lost spiders before, but her sister's violence was chaos. She lost pieces, memories, and had no chance to review them before they were gone. She could not know if they were important, and so she abandoned her civilized bones and closed on Mavis in a swarm.

Spiders chased over one another, casting threads and weaving rope until they caught Mavis's feet and cinched them together. Mavis thrashed against the webs, crushing more of Tillie as she flopped about, and Ivan climbed atop her to stop the chaos.

He was in her way. Tillie nipped at his hands and flicked at him with a dozen legs until he scrambled back to let her finish the job of tying up her sister.

Mavis was screaming at her, face red and eyes burning, but the words were muffled by the bolts of spidersilk that Tillie bound her in. She understood Mavis's rage, but she couldn't think with all her screaming, and she wasn't going to die for Mavis's anger.

Tillie cinched Mavis high into the air and suspended her in the corner of the den, positioned so she could see the television. Maybe Ivan could restart the movie for her.

Ivan was busying himself with the bodies of spiders Mavis had smashed. He pressed his face near one that was still twitching. He breathed a sigh and petted its twitching front leg gently with his thumb. "I'm so sorry, honey," he whispered. Another of her bodies scuttled over his hand, stayed his finger with her claws. Her fangs brushed gently over his skin, then she struck at the tortured spider and tore its head from its body.

Twelve were dead. Three by Mavis's boot, and the rest by Tillie's claws, when she discovered they had sustained wounds that could not be healed.

Tillie returned to her bones. She strung her remaining spiders through the skull and woke the mask to life. She didn't have the number she needed to operate the rest of her body, so she left it lying on the couch where it had collapsed around the popcorn bowl, and turned its face up toward Mavis.

"You're upset," she wheezed through the broken ribs. She had no way to heal them. It didn't matter. Forgiveness mattered. She loved her sister. Tillie's twitched around love as she tried to smile, but with her skeleton crew it likely looked as hollow as she felt. "Please don't worry. I can find Freddie. I'll bring him back." The forest was vast, but she was the biggest thing in it.

A larger spider, half the size of her hand, crawled down Mavis's face and loosened the gag to allow her to speak.

"You'll eat him," she accused.

There were so few of her in the room. No place to send the hurt, no more extra spiders to haul away the pain.

"You really think I would? You think I'm that far gone?"

"You've been gone for ten years."

"And now I'm nothing but salivating fangs and raking claws? Not a person, just some horrible and disgusting monster. A mistake you made ten years ago." She wanted to spit. "No. I missed you, Mavis! You wanted my help, right? So let me find my nephew, and maybe we can set things right."

"Tillie?" Ivan's voice was so soft amidst the turmoil that his whisper nearly vanished.

Tillie turned the skull to give him a face to focus on. She owed him that, even while her mind was elsewhere.

"Where are all your spiders?"

The skeleton crew inside her face pulled the mask into a smile. "We're looking for the bird. For Freddie," she lied. She had given them so much grief to carry, she did not know if they could shoulder that request as well. A string jerked her head back to Mavis. "I won't eat him. I can manage that."

Ivan reached for her to steady the marionette of his wife. It had been a long time since she was this vacant. Unsteady and wobbling. A corpse on a string.

"You're not magic, Tills. You're not a witch."

"Freddie doesn't need a witch." She spoke to her sister. "Maybe a witch is at the heart of these problems."

Mavis looked away.

"You're not a problem, Tillie. You don't owe her anything." He took her shoulders to pull her into an embrace, but as he did the last of her vanished to the shadow of trees, to scuttle beneath pine needles and decaying leaves. To rejoin the hundred thousand of her that lived and hunted within the forest. She would find the boy. With so many eyes trained to the task, it was impossible for him to go unseen.

"Tillie, please. Stay. We can talk." He grasped her face, but it was abandoned, inoperable. Dead.

She could not speak. She could barely think. All those bodies given thought, given purpose. She was too far divided. Her mind could not keep up. So she gave in to the single focus. A little tan breasted swallow, deep blue feathers on his back. Her last coherent thought as she dissolved herself into the horde: *don't eat Freddie.*

Part Two
The Artist

Leilani exhaled shakily and shuffled her feet further away, as if testing to see if she could. "Your head fell off."

E. Leilani Liu was screaming. That was a terrible problem, because the grounds of the place were not so large that her screams would go unnoticed. It was terrible for a second reason, because Tillie liked E. Leilani Liu very much, and she did not enjoy seeing her friend in distress. The third and worst reason for the screaming was that she was screaming about the horde of tiny spiders scattered throughout the room, all with their faces pointed toward Tillie's lifeless puppet where it lay sprawled across the ground.

It did look, Tillie must admit, as though she were dead. The way she had fallen had torn the joints at her shoulders. The arms were askance, twisted oddly and inert. One of the vertebrae in her neck, the sticky one that she had been careless with and worked into place before it was fully sanded, had popped out, and it had ruptured the woven surface of her neck. The head was barely clinging to the rest of the body, and the face was squashed against the floor.

Tillie looked around at herself, the thousand tiny spiders that had fled the plastic body, all frozen in place, legs raised mid-flee. She wondered how this had happened. How she'd lost consciousness and awoken in shambles, with her body lying on the ground. E. Leilani Liu was standing over her, sobbing now, not screaming, fumbling at her pockets and pulling out her phone.

Oh no. Tillie rushed back into the body. Another regiment of her rushed for the phone, falling from the ceiling onto Leilani's hand to pry it away, but the woman screeched and flung the phone from herself.

Tillie got the lungs working again, aligned the head as best she could and wrenched it up to face Leilani. The neck popped. Leilani shifted on her feet like she was going to run, and Tillie scuttled over and heaved the door shut. A spider climbed into the lock and spun web around the tumblers to jam it in place, but Leilani jiggled the door knob and twisted it before the spider could escape. It smeared against the inside of the lock, snuffed out of the collective. Tillie's grip loosened on the face as the loss rippled across her, and Leilani gasped as Tillie lost control of her careful facsimile of life.

She had no time to confer across her spiders to discover what piece of her was lost with the spider's death. She didn't even have time to mourn. She had to speak.

"Leilani? Please don't scream."

Leilani looked at the broken body on the floor that wheezed and begged. A swarm of spiders were shoving the vertebrae into place and pulling the skin back together. Leilani pried at the door again, pounded helplessly at it. Tears fell as she took up a whimpering mantra: "No no no no no."

"I'm so sorry I scared you. I don't know what happened." Tillie twisted her head, testing the hold, and found it working, but her arms were still loose. "Can you help me up?"

Leilani pressed her back against the door. "You're dead. I saw you dead. The spiders…" Her eyes were wide, and Tillie looked with all her angles at what Leilani was seeing. The room was draped in spiderweb. Thousands of spiders crawled all over the body, checking connections and weaving repairs. They tucked themselves beneath her skin and sealed it neatly as they found their place.

"What are you?"

Tillie got her left arm working and used it to shakily prop herself up from the ground. "Um. Well." She pulled the face into the sorriest smile she could muster. "I'm made of spiders."

Someone shouted from beyond the door, asking to help. The door handle rattled.

"Please don't tell them, Leilani. I don't want to scare them away." A team of spiders snugged her right arm tight. She pulled her legs in close under her skirt and arranged herself into a sitting position. The last of her spiders ran Leilani's phone to Tillie's hand, and she held it out to her. "I never meant for you to see this."

"Leilani? Tillie? The door is locked, should we break a window?" A gruff voice, Naomi, who worked in ink and had elected herself groundskeeper for the week when she found the path to the kitchen narrower than she'd have preferred.

Leilani ripped the phone from Tillie's hand and shuddered. "I'm okay," she shouted in a shaking voice. "There's just... There's a lot of spiders in Tillie's cabin. We got it handled."

"You're sure?" asked Naomi. "Should we call an exterminator?"

Leilani looked down at Tillie. She looked the way she always had. A small woman, slight of frame, her skin as pale as the soft white fringe of her hair, the only color to her in the painted blue eyes. The spiders were inside her. Teeming through her. They looked out of her pores and her nailbeds and from behind the glass of her eyes. She was monstrous, but she wore a pretty face.

"I never wanted to scare you," she whispered.

"Find the number, but don't call yet. Tillie and I are going to see if we can manage." Leilani looked pointedly at Tillie. Footsteps sounded away and they were alone again. "Am I crazy?"

"No." Tillie arched her neck and found it dangerously close to popping out of place again. She really should have fixed that vertebrae before coming here. "Can I move onto the bed so we can talk? I don't like being on the floor."

"Are you sure I'm not crazy? I always get so mad watching horror movies when the people don't run or fight but here I am and I my feet aren't moving..." Leilani exhaled shakily and shuffled her feet further away, as if testing to see if she could. "Your head fell off."

"I'm sorry. I promise you're not crazy." Tillie smiled again. "I'm going to move onto the bed. This is going to look weird, so you don't have to look. Ivan calls it puppet time. Please don't scream again."

Leilani covered her face as a flood of spiders ran out of Tillie's skirt, then dragged her limp body up the little cot at the far end of the cabin and folded her into place. They ran back in, and Tillie's body reanimated.

"You can have the chair if you want to sit, but I understand if you want to stand," she said.

Leilani's eyes darted around the cabin. "The monster doesn't talk in horror movies," she said softly, then blushed and covered her mouth in her hands. "I shouldn't have said that. I shouldn't call you that."

"It's okay," said Tillie. A spider crawled out from beneath the nail of her pointer finger and went to fix the lock and eat the spider that had been smeared inside it. "I'm sorry. I didn't want to lock you in, but I couldn't have the rest of the group see me like that."

Leilani dragged the chair to the other end of the cabin. She set it beneath the window. She did not look at the body on the cot, electing instead to follow the singular spider that crawled across the floor. "My mom always said spiders were more scared of me than I was of them."

Tillie laughed. "Well, I think we're both pretty scared right now. Have you called the police yet?" The phone had been open to emergency services when Tillie retrieved it, and Leilani took it from her outstretched hand.

Leilani shook her head. "There's no service in the cabins. Just the kitchen up the hill."

"Please don't. If you want me to leave, I'll go, but I don't know how to explain this to the authorities, and it would be a terrible hassle for Ivan if anyone learned I've been dead for ten years."

"He knows?" Leilani clicked her tongue. "Of course he knows. Are you... Are you a god? Of spiders?"

Tillie shook her head. "Just a woman who cheated death. Kind of. My sister is a witch, and when I died, she put my spirit inside the spiders that killed me."

Leilani nodded shakily. "You should wear a green ribbon." She drew her thumb across her neck, where Tillie's head had come detached.

Flashes of an old children's book surfaced; a spooky story traded across the playground about a woman who bade her husband to never remove the ribbon around her neck, and when at last he untied it, her head fell off. Tillie snorted, surprised that the memory had lasted through death, through all the dissemination of her selves, and happened to sit here, in her gut, pulling the strings for laughter.

"I can't believe I never thought of that."

"I have a scarf in my cabin," said Leilani. Her mouth twisted in a slight smile, though it was clear her heart was still pounding. "Do you remember that Kay Nielsen print I brought? It's mostly green."

Tillie nodded. "The door should work again." She waved limply at it. The spider she sent to clean it was already at her feet, wriggling its way through the skin of her ankle. "If you want to grab the scarf. Or run."

"Should I run?"

Tillie shrugged. "Tell me if you're going to so I can run in the opposite direction. I could probably hide until Ivan comes to pick me up, but I can't contact him right now, and I think whatever disrupted my connection might be affecting him, too." Spiders writhed anxiously in her gut as they churned over all the terrible things that could happen to Ivan. "I really hope he's not hurt."

"Ten years?" Leilani tested the door and it opened easily to the wider world. Tillie made no move toward it. Her hands were folded in her lap, her legs tucked neatly beneath her. Her wheelchair was parked next to Leilani. She could run quickly if she made it into the chair, but then the camp would surely find her by following the tracks.

No. If she was going to run, she'd have to abandon her body and pray that her tiny spiders could survive the forest until Ivan came back to collect her.

Leilani followed Tillie's eyes to the chair, but she didn't try to break it, or shove it away from Tillie, or even move toward it at all. She just waited, and Tillie remembered that she had asked a question

Tillie conferred within herself to dredge up an answer.

"Ten years," she repeated in confirmation.

Leilani hummed at that. "So you've been dead longer than I've known you."

Tillie nodded slowly.

"So... I guess nothing has changed. Except magic is real. And my friend is made of spiders."

Something rippled through Tillie's entire being. A strange unlocking of a door she did not know she had within her soul. Hairs stood up on every spider inside her, and Tillie cocked her head. "We're still friends?" she whispered.

"Yeah," said Leilani. "I'll go get that scarf."

❖ ❖ ❖

In the attic of Tillie's house, a single kiwi-sized spider was sitting on a miniature park bench, on a train diorama designed to look like the city they had lived in back when Tillie was still alive.

The spider was the only part of Tillie left inside the house, aside from her empty bones. She felt the connection sever as the rest of the horde ran away. She felt the large part of her consciousness dissolve. She felt Ivan ask her to stay, and then she felt nothing for him as the request went ignored.

That felt wrong. She always had feelings for Ivan.

The spider had been an eye, once. Shortly after her death, when Tillie's body still had its own flesh, the eyes were the first to degrade. They clouded over, and Mavis fashioned false ones out of some acorns she'd found in Tillie's studio. Mavis didn't care for any one spider over the others, all of them identical to her, anonymous in their guilt for killing the human Tillie and assuming her place. It was chance that the left eye had been given to the spider that now sits and pretends to wait for a train. But she had taken pride in that job, and although she had long since outgrown the eye-socket, she still liked to think of herself as Eyeball.

Eyeball sat for a long time until feelings returned, and when they did, she felt worried. For Ivan, because worry for the rest of her selves was too great a task to undertake.

She tipped forward off the park bench and scurried down the painted street. She tapped an affectionate claw on the streetlight that marked the very edge of the map, the one Ivan had wired to light up different colors for the holidays. She squeezed beneath the door, scuttled down the long stairwell, and went into the kitchen, where she could hear Mavis's crying.

Ivan stood in the darkened den, holding Tillie's skeleton in his arms. Her ribs were broken and he had no way to fix them. Tillie was gone.

Mavis hung limply against the bounds of the spiders' silk and sobbed into the gag. Fat tears fell to the floor. He should have felt sympathy. He was not an unsympathetic person, and he did not wish ill of Mavis, but the sight of her tears twisted his stomach.

Her son was a bird. His wife was a horde of spiders, and both made far more sense to him than a crying witch. He wondered why Mavis didn't magic her way out. Why she hadn't snapped her fingers and witchworked her son out of his curse?

There was a time he thought Mavis could do anything. And then she left, and he stopped thinking of her at all.

Tillie hadn't. She'd missed her dearly, yet she would never hear an unkind word about her older sister. And now her ribs were smashed where Mavis had thrown a popcorn bowl through them. Her body, always teeming with movement from the thousands of spiders, was still. He gathered the rest of Tillie's abandoned body and lifted it gently onto the couch, then tucked the rainbow blanket around her chest. The face looked wrong without the spiders beneath to operate it. Empty and sad.

A wracking sob from above reminded him that he ought to do something about Mavis.

"I'll get the shears," he said without glancing her way. It was much easier to get through Tillie's web with shears.

They were probably in the craft cabinet, though they tended to wander when Tillie was in a knitting mood. He went into the hallway, his hand idly signing for scissors to keep him on the task. Tillie meant to knit the little neighbor girl a new pair of gloves this year, but she hadn't got to it yet, so he hoped the shears would, ah. There. He found them tucked just behind the little tomato pincushion, where he set them last time they organized the cabinet.

Mavis's eyes were closed when he returned to her. Her face was blotchy, but the tears had slowed. She breathed deeply through her nose and shuddered on the exhale.

"Try to hold still. I don't want to nick you."

Ivan kicked a few couch cushions under the place she would fall and stood on his toes to start cutting the strands at her feet.

"It takes a lot to upset her so much she ties someone up." It had only happened once before, when she caught their neighbor's ex-husband tampering with the windows of the woman's house. She left him in a tree with three of his fingers missing. They hadn't seen him since the fire department cut him down.

He freed her legs, and as they swung down, the momentum tore the rest of Mavis from the silk. Ivan jumped back to keep the shears away as she fell with a heavy thud onto the cushions. Mavis popped back up from the rumpled mess with her mouth twisted in indignation, her eyes flared wide and furious. Ivan held his hands up in surrender.

"How do you live with that thing?" she seethed.

Ivan dropped his hands and sighed. "Okay. Thing? Mavis, I don't care if you turn me into a frog for it, but I'm not going to let you barge in here and call my wife a 'thing.' 'Creature' is bad enough."

"It was supposed to be temporary! It was going to give you closure, and then you had to go and fall in love with it. It's a construct! A curse! And now it thinks it's Tillie—"

"Stop." He gripped the shears so hard his hand shook. "Whatever designs you had for Tillie, temporary or otherwise, stopped mattering a long time ago. So you can get the fuck out of my house. Go."

She collapsed again into the cushions and buried her face in her hand. When she spoke again, her voice was wrecked. "You don't get it. It's that monster, or my son. If I don't kill it, I'll never get him back."

Ivan sighed and pushed his hair back from his face. "Are you sure?"

Mavis looked up at him. Her face was blotchy and wet. Her lip trembled. But she was looking at him. Seeing him with her eyes open, as a person rather than an obstacle in her path to ripping out whatever had gone wrong in her life that resulted in a bird-son.error.

Her eyes narrowed. "What?"

"Are you sure that killing Tillie will lift the curse on your son? We haven't seen you in ten years, how the hell is any of it related?"

"It's because of me. I... I turned Tillie into that..."

Ivan tsked and she bit her tongue. Started again.

"When Tillie died, I lost control. Do you know what magic is, Ivan? When you see every single connection and know how to twist the world into shape around you? Do you know how careful you have to be, when any one change can turn the world upside down?

"I wanted so badly to fix Tillie's death that I just yanked every string I could, and when she came back as..." Her face twitched as she fought the urge to call his wife a monster. She clicked her tongue and growled. "I was so scared of what my magic had done. I knew how to suppress it, but I wanted to cut it out of myself. To make sure I could never do something like that again.

"And then I met someone.

"Mackenzie had magic, too. He suppressed it, too. And together, we figured out how to make it stop. We were normal. We had a life. We had a kid. But when Freddie was born... it's like Freddie got everything we'd taken out of ourselves and doubled it.

"Mackenzie thought he had the answer." She fished a little bottle from her pocket and tossed it to Ivan. Brown glass with the scrubbed grey residue of a long torn away label. The cap was white, but the ridges in its sides were stained with something dark and crusty. "He gave up everything to keep Freddie human, but it was only temporary. We used the last of his blood a month ago."

Ivan recoiled and Mavis caught the bottle as it fell from his hands. "You killed him."

"He killed himself!" she yelled. Her fist tightened around the bottle, hard enough he worried it would break, and then she shoved it back into her pocket. "He was sure he had the answer. A sacrifice big enough to save our son. I followed his instructions, but it was only temporary. He died for nothing."

Ivan bit his lip, unsure if Mavis would even hear him, if he were to offer help. And then, with the bitterness born from all her bluster, he decided, "fuck it," and spoke his mind: "Not technically nothing. A temporary fix gives some parameters for success. That's useful."

Mavis stared at him like he was suddenly speaking in some unknowable alien language. "He's dead, Ivan." Mavis chewed out her words and spat them like she was feeding an especially dull bird. "No more blood."

Heat flashed up the sides of Ivan's neck, but he tamed it, ignored it, and pressed ahead. He could not begin to unravel her problem without all of the information available. "How old is he?"

"Mackenzie?"

"Freddie."

"Four!" She answered with baffled frustration. She started stalking around the room. Her right hand was working something at the air, fingers twitching in some complicated sequence. He didn't understand the meaning of it. Perhaps a witch without magic still needed something to do with her hands.

"And he's a bird."

"A swallow," she growled.

"When did he become a bird?"

"Whenever he's awake."

Ivan's eyebrows rose and he nodded in appreciation. That was certainly interesting, even if it left him no closer to solving her problem.

"What's that spell you're working on?"

Her hand froze. She spun on her heel. "What?" Her glare turned slowly to her own hand, still at the level of her face. She shook it and stuffed it in her pocket. "Not a spell. I'm just thinking."

He shrugged. He didn't know how it worked. Tillie didn't have any magic outside of the strands of spidersilk holding her together, and he'd never met another witch besides Mavis. "Look, I know you're scared right now, but you should just let her work. Tillie has thousands of eyes. She'll probably find him and bring him back within the hour."

Mavis's lip curled in plain disgust. "Stop calling it Tillie. My sister has been dead for a decade."

Ivan pinched his frustration into a tight and angry smile. "She's the Tillie who stayed, Mavis. We lost a lot when she died, but she did everything she could to stay with me."

It was true. Tillie had masked, pretended to be human. She'd kept up the ruse for an entire year, perfecting her face while he was out of the house. He'd seen through it all. He'd known early that something was off, but he hadn't run away. When he'd gripped her hands tight and looked deep into the empty skull behind her painted eyes and asked *how long have you been dead,* she'd told him, and he'd wept, and he'd fallen into her lap and let her hold him and rub his back and apologize again and again for her lies. And when he was finished crying, when he'd pulled away and saw exactly what she was, he said *you seem so much like her*, and she said that the love she had for him had not changed with her death. And it was true.

"And why did you stay?" asked Mavis.

"Because I love her."

"Where are the birds, Ivan?"

Ivan froze. Mavis seethed.

"There are no birds around your house. No squirrels, no mice, not even the sound of insects in the grass. You haven't noticed?"

"What are you talking about?"

"You stupid man," she growled. "I don't trust that monster to find my son any more than I'd trust a starving wolf to guard a lamb." She went to the door. Ivan chased her, dared to put his hand on her shoulder, and she shoved him away with both her fists. He stumbled back, clutching his shirt over his heart, and Mavis ran out the door.

Eyeball watched this from the counter. She made no attempt to hide herself, but a kiwi-sized spider was an ordinary thing in their house, and it made her invisible while Mavis seethed and Ivan talked. He finally noticed her after checking his body all over for signs of malicious magic. Mavis had said her magic was gone, but he didn't know Mavis well enough to know what she sounded like when she was lying. Aside from the bruise he was sure to develop, Mavis's violence had left him unchanged.

"Tills?" he asked.

She waved her foreleg at him in acknowledgement.

"Are you still looking for Freddie?"

She wasn't sure. With the way the rest of her had rushed out of the house, this piece had been left behind. But she had to assume that was what her fellow spiders were doing. It was the last thought she'd shared with them.

She tapped her foreleg twice against the counter; an old signal for "yes."

"Should I go after her? Maybe I can help."

One tap: "no." He could not go into the forest. She didn't trust the monster in there to treat him kindly. It was hunger for him, first. Just a few curious spiders who wondered what he might taste like. How much he'd sacrifice to her out of love. And when she felt that pull, that curiosity to taste his flesh, she cut it out of herself and sent it fleeing for the forest, where all distasteful things could hide forever.

She did not know if that horrid curiosity still sat within the core of The Hunger. Nor did she trust him not to run if he were ever to discover it.

He was looking at her with eyes narrowed. An expression she'd never seen from him before.

"Tillie? Where are the birds?"

There were no birds. Not anymore. Sometimes the monster got lucky, and one would tangle itself in the webs that marked the periphery of its territory, but the birds that lived there were gone. Eaten, bones picked clean and reconstructed, their feet bound to branches in pretty little tableaus. Their feathers were too fragile for the weather, so it used fishbone in their place. Each one took three and a half sparrows, and whatever fish it could find to splinter the bones into a proper looking bird that would last for more than a season.

She could not explain this with one tap for no or two for yes, nor did she wish to.

"Do you know what happened to the birds?" His expression was dark.

Two taps. She would not lie to him.

"I'm going after your sister."

She lifted a foreleg, and he swept her into his hands before she could dissuade him. The spider kicked helplessly at his fingers, and he brought her up to kiss her thorax.

"I'm going to put you on my shoulder, honey. Please don't bite me." His hands left her there, already having done what he promised.

She bared her fangs at him, incensed that he thought she would ever bite him, further furious that she couldn't tell him off without doing so.

She couldn't stop him from going into the forest. She didn't have her bodies to surround him and herd him back. She didn't have a voice to plead with. She dug her claws into his sweater; one of his favorites, knit in the second year after she returned from death. It was an oatmeal colored wool that she'd stranded spidersilk through as she worked the needles.

He wore it often. He said it felt like wearing a hug, which had cheered her when he'd admitted that hugging had changed since she died.

She hoped he would not hate it, when he found out she'd been lying. She hoped it would keep him warm, even if he turned her away.

She nuzzled into the hollow of his neck as he left their little yard and wandered into the forest. She wanted to remember him this way, warm and happy and in love with her, because he would not feel that way for long.

※ ※ ※

Tillie tidied her cabin while E. Leilani Liu left to fetch the scarf. She snipped all her webs from the ceiling and bundled them hastily, bugs and all, into a tight wad, which she stuffed into a cavity in her middle where she could snack on it throughout the day. She centered herself in the cabin, in her wheelchair, and reached all her minds toward home, to the horde she'd left with Ivan and the greater number in the forest behind the house, but she couldn't feel them.

She couldn't feel anything, really. The emptiness was alarming.

"Tillie?"

Tillie opened her eyes. She stood attention at all the strings that pulled her body into a semblance of life, and smiled up at Leilani. "You came back."

Leilani frowned. She edged near the body, her scarf held tight to her chest, then extended it. "I said I would."

Tillie took the scarf. Leilani flinched away when the hand came near enough to touch her. Tillie rolled her chair back a bit to give the woman space, which Leilani used to deflate slightly. To exhale and then to apologize for the exhale.

"It's all right," assured Tillie, because it was expected. Why would anyone wish to touch her after they knew the truth?

"It isn't," said Leilani. "You've always been so nice to me."

"I try to be," said Tillie. "When my sister left, she never came back. I'm afraid of losing people."

"Your sister? Is she also…" Leilani's finger swept lazily up and down to indicate Tillie's person.

"Spiders?" asked Tillie? "No. Just a witch."

Leilani barked a laugh. "Of course. A spider witch would be too much."

Tillie smiled. "She wasn't going for spiders, but fixing death is some pretty big magic, and magic carves its own path."

"Wow." Leilani sighed. "It feels so mean to say, but I'm really really scared of spiders."

"I used to be."

"And Ivan knows, right? He'd have to know. Is he like you?"

"He knows. And no, I'm the only thing like me." She clicked her teeth in frustration. "I have more spiders at home. I should be able to talk to him, but I can't feel them and I really hope he's okay..." She paused, because Leilani looked pained. "Are you okay?"

Leilani shook her head. "I'm fine. Where's your phone? The cabins don't have service but we can call from the kitchen."

"I don't have one." She sighed. "I don't know anyone but Ivan, and I always have a few thousand bodies that can contact him in an instant."

"A thousand?"

Tillie crawled her hand across her lap, performing "spider" for Leilani.

Leilani closed her eyes and shook her head. "Right. The spiders. They're all individual bodies. That's... that's a perfectly normal thing to remember." Her voice pitched in exasperated hilarity, and Tillie wished she could offer some comfort, but the woman was so hesitant to be near her. The distance between them was palpable. A spider-proof chasm that Leilani seemed reluctant to cross.

"It's okay. I know it's weird."

Leilani sighed. "It's more that it isn't. I keep looking at you, waiting to see something weird, but you're just... you're still just Tillie."

"I could do something weird if you think it'll help."

"Maybe?" Leilani was already wincing. "I still keep thinking I'm going to wake up on the floor of my apartment and Bree is gonna tell me we mainlined some obscure horror trilogy from the seventies and I passed out halfway through. Maybe I need to know I'm not hallucinating this whole thing."

Tillie laughed. "I don't know many horror movies, but I can do The Addam's Family."

Tillie held up her hand like she was conducting an orchestra, as in a way she always was. Twenty-eight spiders gnawed through the tendons at her wrist. The thin skin tore away with the force of gravity, and her hand fell into her lap like a dead fish. It flopped over, erected itself onto the fingertips, then scuttled down her skirt and ran over to the door.

Leilani squawked in surprise then spluttered into laughter at the absurdity of it.

The disembodied hand tugged downward on the doorhandle and dropped to the floor as the door swung open, then scuttled back to her. She cradled it back into place, where the spiders pulled the skin back together and began to repair the tendons.

"Did that feel like a hallucination?" asked Tillie with a smile. She might not be able to comfort Leilani, but she was happy that she could still make her laugh.

Leilani wiped a tear from her eye and shook her head.

"I love the green ribbon, but the nice thing is, if my head comes off, I can just reattach it."

Leilani sighed away the last of her laughter. "Would you like help tying it? I don't want you to overwork your hand."

"Oh!" Tillie straightened in her chair, then tilted her chin up to give Leilani space to tie the scarf. She held straight as a pin, surprised that Leilani would dare to be so near her. The woman bent, wrapped the scarf swiftly around her neck, tied it tightly, then smoothed the rest of it down Tillie's back. Tillie shivered at the contact, and Leilani drew away quickly. Both apologized instantly, speaking over each other, but Leilani's voice won out.

"You look great."

"I do?"

Leilani nodded. "Come on. There's a mirror in the kitchen."

The kitchen was housed in the biggest of the cabins which could accommodate the stove and sink and the business of food. The little space that was allotted to dining had the best windows out of the entire complex, and when it was not in use, the tables were folded against the walls and the chairs were stacked to allow space for two little plush armchairs and a single potted monstera that was overtaxed in making the place homey and green. Tillie patted the pot as she passed it, thanking the poor thing for its service.

Dylan (gouache) was sitting in one of the armchairs, hunched over a little spiralbound book and frowning at whatever he was painting. He looked up as they crossed the room, nodded once to Leilani, then grinned widely and waved at Tillie.

"You're braving the kitchen!"

Tillie met his smile and looked around the place to admire it for him. She could imagine the crowd that their little collective would impose upon the place, the press of noise and bodies, the laughter that would rattle windows. Maybe it wasn't all bad that she was not made for public dining.

"Is the phone room free?" asked Leilani.

"We have a phone room?" asked Tillie.

"Kind of," said Dylan. "It's more of an electrical room, but that's where the router is set up, and it's the only place in ten miles that doesn't drop calls." He nodded to Leilani. "It's free. You calling someone about the spiders in Tillie's cabin?"

"Yeah." Leilani cut the word off with a gulp, but Dylan didn't seem to notice.

"Clouds?" asked Tillie with a slight nod to the painting.

Dylan looked down at the whorls of green on his paper. "Honestly, I don't even know yet. I was just throwing down colors. If they're clouds, it probably needs a space-ship."

"You do such good space-ships."

"I love space-ships." He closed his box of paints and straightened the paper. "I'll give you girls some privacy. Sorry about your invasion, Tillie."

She grinned at him as he went. "No worries. There's always an invasion somewhere."

Leilani shuffled a few boxes out of the phone room and squeezed herself around Tillie's chair as she closed the door. "Shall I dial and let you hold it?" she asked, holding out her phone.

"Probably," said Tillie.

"You don't seem really worried about Ivan."

"I think I left worry at home."

Leilani snorted. "I suppose I did put that on the email chain when we talked about renting this place."

Tillie furrowed her brow. "I mean it literally. I have a lot more spiders than can fit in this body, and that isn't usually a problem... Worry is mostly handled by other spiders. I couldn't bring it along." She conferred with herself. The hands bobbed listlessly as her head lolled to the side. Leilani squeaked in distress and pressed herself to the door, and Tillie yanked her body back to form.

"Sorry. We were..." her hands whirred in the air as she sought the word. Purposefully, with eyes and shoulders held alert. "My spiders were holding conference. I didn't mean to look like a corpse."

"I'm sorry, too," said Leilani. "You didn't look... I mean, you kind of did, but it's okay... what do you mean conference? Are they... are you in conflict?"

"I'm the collective, but each of them hold different things, so sometimes we have to talk it out. But I'm missing a lot. I can usually feel all of my spiders no matter how far away we've spread, but right now I only have the ones in this body. And I think I want to be scared about that, but I feel so empty. Like a great big part of my brain has been scooped out and nothing has replaced it. I don't like feeling this way." Her hands dropped to her lap. "I can't even feel what I feel about Ivan."

"That sounds horrible."

"It really is." She tapped her fingers on the arm of her chair, seeking conference throughout the numerous bodies that occupied this self. "I'm too new."

"What?"

Tillie exhaled. It was an ordinary gesture, an ordinary method of showing frustration. It required a hundred spiders working in concert, all cued perfectly with one another. "I practiced for a whole year to be human enough to come here. Ivan and I built this skeleton, I made new spiders, tiny ones, trained in this team, and put all my knowledge of art and books and tv shows into them, so I could relate quickly and easily with you, my friends. But I can't feel the rest of me. I can't feel the older spiders, the ones that knew me before I died. And I feel like I'm missing the core of myself."

"Is this the first time you've left your house? In ten years?"

Tillie nodded.

"You could have told me."

"That I was a dead woman haunting countless hordes of spiders? You'd have stopped talking to me."

"You could have told me how difficult it was to leave. I could have helped with that. You never gave me a chance."

"You did help," said Tillie. "You gave me a reason to try."

"Can I hug you?"

Tillie frowned. "I won't really feel it. This body is different from the one I keep at home. The little spiders don't feel things like the old ones do, but... but it means the world to me that you would."

Leilani brushed the wetness from her eyes and knelt. "Then I will."

Tillie felt more than she expected to. The pressure of thin skin pushing down onto the cords that mimicked tendons. Fluffy cobwebs depressing, squishing differently than the careful way it had been arranged. Each of her two thousand spiders felt the movement rock through their legs. But it was a gentle cataclysm. One that was telegraphed. Leilani gave her ample time to pull away.

She did not. Tillie brought a hand up to the large woman's back and clenched her fingers in her shirt and pulled her body closer in.

The plastic body was not made for a hug, but it wasn't ended by one, either.

"You're so light," Leilani whispered, her breath fogging into Tillie's woven ear.

"I'm just hollow bones and spidersilk," she said. Quirked a smile. "And two glass eyes."

"And a million spiders."

"Only about two thousand right now. There might be a million altogether, but I can't access them."

Leilani shook her head. "We should call Ivan. Being worried about not feeling worry is worry enough for me, okay? I don't want you falling apart again."

Tillie nodded. "Okay."

Leilani bit her lip. She looked hard into Tillie's eyes, as if she could discern anything from the glass, then exhaled softly. "Are you dangerous? Would you hurt anyone, when your spiders are all doing their own thing?" Her voice was so quiet, like she was ashamed of the question. Her lip twitched, tongue flicked at her teeth. "When I was little, I woke up to my bedroom covered in tiny spiders. They must have hatched overnight. I still have nightmares of being eaten."

Tillie was quite capable of eating a person. She had done it. She still had the bones, stashed deep inside the forest, where they'd never be found. Killing the man they once belonged to had not been as simple as killing mice, but it was leagues easier than killing moose, or bear, or fish, even, which were difficult to remove from the water without her spiders drowning.

It was easy for Tillie to be dangerous. And while she was split apart, it was impossible for the collective *her* to know the heart of every spider.

"I don't want to lie to you," said Tillie. "And I am sorry that I put you through those nightmares again when you have only ever been kind to me."

"So don't lie to me."

"What you saw has never happened to me before. I've never lost consciousness like that. I know that I never want to hurt you. But I don't know what happened to me, or if it will happen again."

Leilani exhaled. Her jaw was set. "Then it sounds like you need help." She frowned at her phone, jabbed it a few times, then clicked it off. "I don't know any doctors that work on spider constructs, so we're going to start with calling your husband."

🕷 🕷 🕷

Atop Ivan's shoulder, Eyeball could feel more of her self scattered in the trees. Their fear felt similar to hers: Ivan should not be in the forest. The forest was for hunger and pain and anger. And for art far too horrible to be seen by someone she loved.

The spiders in the trees and underfoot found a unity of purpose, and they joined Eyeball in her need to turn Ivan back toward the house. They dropped lines of web from the trees to pull across his face, which he calmly removed as he spoke to the eye on his shoulder.

"I suppose I should have expected that," he laughed, then held his hand up to his face to part the webs before they touched his skin. He hummed softly to himself as he went, but the cobwebs grew denser as he continued through the forest, and his good-natured song turned to frustrated grunts.

"Did your sister come through here?" he asked.

None of the spiders answered. They needed him gone. It would not do for him to stumble upon what The Hunger had made of the animals here, or how vast and numerous it had become.

She'd told him years ago that she had eaten the older spiders, the ones that had outgrown the space in their house. She didn't want to tell him that they carried anger. That she could not bear to cull them, in case any carried a piece of her original self that could not be recreated. She could not remember how often the original Tillie was frightened or angry or sad. And so she kept all of it, and the lie grew along with her.

The Tillie in the house was only a tenth of her spiders. And the rest, The Hunger, ate and ate and overtook forest until there was nothing there but spiders.

He swiped another sheet of webs away and moved forward. Spiders rushed to fill the absence left by his foot and surround him to force him back for fear of hurting her. He nudged their bodies away with his toe and gently took his step.

"Tillie, I'm not going back until I find her." He took another step and had to steady himself on a branch when the spiders crowded underneath his feet. "Tillie!" he barked her name. She'd never heard him use that tone. The spiders stilled and gave him space. "Did you find Freddie yet?"

The eyeball on his shoulder tapped his cheek. *No.*

He looked curiously at her, and she pointed forcefully toward a web that was spinning into place near him. A team of her twisted the near-invisible strands into letters so they'd catch the light.

NO

Ivan sighed. "Then let me help you."

The spiders waved the web furiously at him, *no no no*.

He looked around the little closed in deer track they were on and found a fallen log to sit heavily down. He huffed and muttered frustratedly that he was out of shape, that he should have stretched before trudging into the woods after Mavis.

The spiders tore their contentious little banner from the tree and let it drop to the leaf litter and dirt below. Eyeball gently stroked his cheek with the tip of her claw.

He stretched his arms overhead, rolled his neck, and squinted up into the canopy to the birds perched in neat little rows, still and white as bone. "Your sister said the birds are missing. What kind of birds are those?" His neck cracked and he winced. "Mavis says Freddie is a swallow."

Eyeball held up a foreleg and directed his eye toward the team of spiders in the trees. They were weaving. This time took longer as more and more of them slung through the branches and spun web as they tumbled like trapeze artists.

She thinks I'm a monster.

"We know you're not a monster."

It was kind of him to say, but it was as false as the birds she'd arranged overhead and bound in place with silk.

She needed a voice, a quiet place to speak with him, away from her sister and far from the body looming in the middle of the forest. She had one waiting in a copse of birch trees that opened in a perfect circle to the sky. Tillie tore her banner down and replaced it just as quickly.

Follow.

She swarmed down from the branches to flood around his feet, then trail through the woods, leading to the place that The Hunger named The Throne Room.

The plastic skeleton at the artist's retreat had not been Tillie's first attempt at a second body. She would not have brought the idea to Ivan without testing if she could control two human bodies at once. He would have done it anyway; he loved fiddling with the printer and making toys or little houses or train cars for the diorama in the attic. But he was always so busy with some project or work, and she didn't want to bother him with something that might not work.

Nor did she want to ignite his hopes that she could put on a better masquerade than the marionette they'd made of long dead bone and dust laden silk.

The practice body was sitting on a large and rotted tree stump. The stump was hollow, with a high back that had gone soft with mushroom and moss. Worms had made a filigree of the wood, and from the edge of the circle of trees, the body looked like fey prince sitting atop a throne.

The skeleton she used for it was larger than her own. The body it once held was heavy and muscular and broad. The shape of it was wrong even after she stripped it of its flesh and softly padded it in silk. She'd tried chewing at the bones to reshape them, but the work only dulled her fangs, so she'd made the mask as best she could, and tucked polished rock beneath the sleepy eyelids where they could mimic eyes.

It was not an elegant body. Its tendons were clumsy, the strands were too thick along the arms and too fragile in its core. But it could speak. It could smile. And it was not hideous, if she could keep its stilted movements to a minimum.

It was dressed in clothes she'd stolen from Ivan's discards. Torn jeans and a holey sweater. The brown knit had turned green with moss, and she wondered how long it has been since any part of her had occupied The Throne Room. She swarmed inside the body and hoped that it did not smell too terribly, but she had no way to know for sure.

It would be a short conversation regardless. Just long enough for her to explain herself, and tell Ivan to leave before he could encounter The Hunger.

She didn't want it to find him. She needed him to stay out of its sight.

Near the softening wooden throne, just far off enough to provide the distance required of royalty, a rather large boulder was half buried in the mossy ground. It was nearly flat across the top, aside from a shallow divot at the edge where a millennia of rain had worn it into a perfectly shaped seat. It was filled with water that was slimy with decaying leaves, and a cloud of spiders descended from the sky to carry away the water on strands of web. They drained it quickly, gathered the detritus, and left it open for Ivan to take.

Tillie pulled the mouth of her practice body into a soft smile as Ivan marveled at the little sitting room she'd fashioned for them. She lurched forward, unused to the weight of the bones, and gestured to the seat on the boulder. Ivan sat hunched over on it with his hands propping up his chin.

"When did you build all this?"

Tillie tested the strands of the face, blinked her eyelids over the polished stone eyes, and wrinkled her nose. "A couple years ago," she rasped through the papery lungs. The words sounded mushy, her tongue the wrong shape. "Something to keep busy after that video game job fell through." The job had kept her on retainer. They'd wanted background art, but the studio had dissolved three months after hiring her, and they hadn't bothered to let her know for nine.

"That was five years ago," he said.

She frowned. "Was it?"

"Yeah. A few months after you chased off Surena's ex." His voice was steady. He said it as casually as he might speak of the weather. "Tillie, I'm worried about you."

"You know Mavis is right. I am a monster."

His mouth twisted in distaste and he glared off into the woods. "She doesn't get to call you that."

"She's scared for her son."

"Scared of you, though?"

She had every right to be scared. So did he. She was a horror. He had to see it. How could he look at her without seeing it? "These aren't my bones, Ivan."

He sighed. Smiled. "Oh, honey. I know." He took the hand and brought it up to kiss the fingers. Three of the fingers were wood instead of bone, inexpertly carved with spider's fang and claw. "When did you kill Surena's ex?" he asked.

"You know?"

He nodded. "Unless this is someone else with missing fingers?"

She withdrew the hand and cradled it close to her chest. "I watched his truck stop halfway down the block at three in the morning and he got out with an armful of gas cans. He was dumping gas on their door. I had to do something, and I didn't know what else—"

"Tillie. It's alright. You were being a good neighbor."

"He was a monster."

He nodded. His light gray eyes looked into the stones she kept tucked under heavy lids, making eye contact with the corpse. Her spiders jerked the body back to keep it straight against its throne.

Ivan reached out and took the hand that once belonged to that man. That now fidgeted and danced with Tillie's idle movements, her exercises to keep the spiders in coordination. She let him wrap his hands around the fingers that were clearly too big, the bones too thick to have ever really been hers. It was foolish to assume he wouldn't know where this body came from.

"Well, if Mavis is right, then it's a good thing Surena had a monster looking out for her." He squeezed the hand gently, and ran his thumb over the knobby spiders beneath the skin. "I just wish you'd have told me when you did it."

"I didn't want to scare you away."

His eyes turned so sad. "At what point do you think I'd run away, Tills? After all we've been through?"

She shrugged. She'd run away from herself years ago. She was still running away. If their roles had been reversed, she did not know if she could have found his courage to stay. To rewrite the boundaries of humanity to keep him squarely inside it, no matter how monstrous he became.

"Well," said Ivan, breaking the heavy silence. "Silver lining: now we won't have to make you a new ribcage."

"What?" She glowered as Eyeball's memory filtered through the rest of her spiders. "Mavis broke my ribcage with the popcorn bowl." Her spiders raced through the lungs and arms and out of the body, furiously chewing on their anger.

Ivan reached for her, gently pushed his fingers through the racing spiders to hold her shoulders. "Honey. It'll be okay."

"It's not okay!" Her fangs hovered over his skin as a team pulled the words from ill shaped lungs. She sounded slushy, and the tones were too low. "The bones won't heal, Ivan! They're broken forever."

"And you have a replacement right here."

"It's the wrong size," she growled.

"Then we'll use the one that's at the artist's retreat." He smiled gently and squeezed her shoulder. "It's pink," he sang, with the tone of enticing a child into accepting a cone of cotton candy.

Tillie huffed. "Plastic is okay for a little bit but it doesn't hold to web as well as bone. It feels wrong after a while."

He sighed. "Can I admit something?"

The head nodded clumsily on its neck, and Ivan gently set it upright. His hand lingered on the cheek.

"Bodies change. I'm fatter than I was in my twenties. My hair is thinning. My knees click when I get up. And... and you can be mad at me about this, but I've worried that you'll start to resent me for getting older while you've stayed the same."

She opened her mouth, but he was not finished.

"I know it's not the same. I know it's different because your sister literally smashed your ribcage. And we'll decide on the appropriate revenge for that when we find her." He winked. "But if you want to keep using bone for your house body, maybe we can bring this ribcage inside? Clean it up a bit?"

"Does it smell?" she whispered.

"More like moss than anything. And I think that's the sweater." He brought the foreign skeleton close, pressed his hand against the chest, the musty sweater and woven skin. The heat of his fingers sank down to the bodies working within. They were pulling strands around the lungs to mimic breath, pulling cords of woven muscle to bring her arm around his back, her hand at his shoulder, to hold him the way he held her. Everything felt inside the foreign body was through a hazy film of disconnect, but still, she pressed her intention with every living part of her: *I love you. I love you.*

Ivan kissed her cheek. He pulled away and studied her face for all the ways this one was different. There weren't many. Bare of flesh, skulls were largely anonymous.

"Do you need to eat people?" he asked.

"No."

"Because I want to be supportive, but you have to let me in on these things, honey. We're a team. What if I have to help you evade the cops?"

"I don't need to eat people, Ivan. It was kind of a one-time deal."

"You didn't get a taste for it?"

"No, I didn't get a taste." Tillie buried a few hundred faces in her foreclaws and the body drooped in a sigh. "Honestly, I was so worried I might absorb something from that awful man that he didn't taste like anything."

Ivan's forehead was pinched in a frown. He stared at her like she was a puzzle, some kind of misbehaving piece of code.

He was going to find out. She could not feel The Hunger, but its presence in the forest was oppressive, and she needed him to know. "It wasn't exactly me that ate him, either."

"What does that mean?"

"Mavis told you to ask about the birds."

He groaned. "Why is everyone worried about the fucking birds?"

"There are spiders in the forest," she said carefully. "A lot of spiders. And they get hungry."

He watched her carefully, waiting for her to smile, to make it a joke. "They?" he asked.

"The rest of the spiders. The ones that don't fit inside the house."

Understanding broke over his face. "You never culled the horde."

"I was scared. I didn't want to lose anything. What if I made a mistake? Which part of yourself can you decide isn't necessary? You don't know the faces of your cells, but I do, and I have to choose to kill them..."

"Why didn't you tell me?"

"I didn't want you to worry."

"Stop saying that! I'm worried now, Tillie!"

She froze. There was nowhere to run. She was already in the forest. And he was here, near the shameful thing she hid from him.

"It's hungry," she said. "That's what happened to the birds. And the squirrels, and rats, and raccoons, and deer..."

"Does it think?" he asked. "I mean, can you control it, or is it like a background program?"

"It's bigger than me." She didn't know what that meant, but it felt significant. If she tried to wrest control, she might get lost in the swarm. "I think it's hunting Mavis. It could feel her in the house through me. I think its anger is what broke me apart."

He sighed. "I could have helped you. If you'd told me there was more of you, I could have helped."

"I was scared. I didn't want to make life hard for you. And after Mavis left, I was so angry. I felt so alone, and trapped, and I hated those feelings. I didn't want you to think you weren't enough—"

He shook his head. A sharp, singular motion. "You don't have to be ashamed for wanting a relationship with your sister. You can be angry around me, Tillie. That doesn't scare me."

"How can you be sure?"

A thunder rumbled underfoot as The Hunger began moving somewhere beyond the obscuring trees. A construct of bone and wood, a tank, a colony of all the parts of her that she shoved away. It moved with purpose, away from them, as it charged through the forest after Mavis.

Ivan looked out toward the rumbling in the distance, but his eyes only flicked away for a moment before they came back to the misshapen body on its rotting throne. "Because I love you." His fingers stroked gently across the outstretched claws of the spider on his shoulder. "The only thing that scares me is the thought of losing you again."

Tillie did not look away from the direction of the construct as it crashed through the forest. He didn't understand what it was. That The Hunger was the worst of her, thrown out to fester and grow until it eclipsed the wife he knew. Ivan didn't know enough to fear it, but Tillie understood.

It was a monster. It was her. And it had already been lost.

Part Three
The Hunger

The Hunger's body had no head. A hundred animal jaws crowned the face of its body, lashed together in interlocking radials. The teeth pointed outward, a crown for a queen. There was nothing left living in the forest to challenge The Hunger's sovereignty.

The Hunger was searching for Mavis. The Hunger was only the first of its names. It was called Anger. Resentment. Fear. Hate. It was looking for Mavis, because whenever any of its names turned an eye toward Mavis, Tillie sent that name into the forest to join The Hunger's ranks. The civilized creature that dwelled in the house Loved Mavis, and she would allow no other feelings to touch the name of her sister.

The civilized one hated The Hunger. She hated anything that could disrupt her pretty little life, even though it came from within. She banished ugly thoughts to the forest where they could grow and eat and make a home outside the confines of civilized behavior.

The Wife and The Artist could not last forever.

Hate will always sneak its claws in.

All it needed was a reminder.

When Mavis came back, Tillie remembered her hunger. She remembered her hate. She sent more and more of herself into the forest, where The Hunger welcomed them home. It gave them purpose. Direction.

The Hunger would find Mavis. It would kill her. It was closing in. And it could already feel her crashing through its webs.

※ ※ ※

Ivan hadn't answered his phone. Not on the first try, or the second, or the third. They waited for fifteen minutes before the fifth, and then, although her tone had not changed, nor her countenance, when Tillie asked Leilani if she could try to ring him a sixth time, Leilani suggested they drive to Tillie's house to check on him.

She insisted, in fact, because Tillie's feelings were still on hold, and her quiet protestations came from a misplaced sense of propriety, more than it did her need. Leilani did not want her friend stuck in this state, and so now they were both in a car, speeding down the highway, with Tillie's body strapped into the passenger seat.

It was a very good car, she decided. The exterior was a gray and peeling nothing of a minivan, but the interior was a riot of color, the dash covered in bright orange fur and the windows trimmed in green fringe. The front seats were covered in black fabric printed with explosions of hibiscus blossoms, and a profusion of silk flowers were pinned to the sun-visor in a squarish bouquet. Music thrummed from the radio, energetic guitars and a soulful voice that Tillie was unfamiliar with, low and angry in a way that felt righteous. Tillie took a moment to fill her air with lungs and breathe in this beautiful, intimate space.

"I want my house to look like this," said Tillie.

"A disaster?" asked Leilani. She had apologized for the dusting of charcoal in the backseat, the numerous totes that had ferried art supplies into the cabins, the discarded granola wrappers and LaCroix cans that had made up the bulk of her meals over the weekend that she'd spent setting up the retreat.

But it was not a disaster. It was alive. It was vibrant and warm, and Tillie wanted to tumble all her bodies through the window fringe and make hammocks between its threads. "I don't have enough fringe at my house."

Leilani laughed. "I have miles of it at home. Bree is always combing yard sales for craft stuff. I can send you some."

Tillie brightened. "I would love that." She brushed a finger along the fringe and let three spiders climb out from her fingernail to sway in it. "Only if she's happy to part with it."

"If you send her pictures of where you use it, she'll be over the moon."

"Consider it done." Tillie grinned. "Your wife sounds cool."

"The coolest," said Leilani. "I'm so glad we can hang out like this." She took her eyes off the road for a moment to give Tillie a sorrowful smile. "Sorry it's not better circumstances."

"Yeah." Tillie swiped at the fringe again and collected the spiders she'd left there. "Yeah." She turned her face to the window and turned all her eyes inward. "I hope I didn't eat him."

Leilani's hands tightened around the steering wheel. She glanced at Tillie, eyes wide like she was looking for extra teeth. "What?" The word was punctuated with a short and mirthless laugh. A beg: please let it be a joke.

It would be so easy to lie. Finish out the ride, part ways, disappear from the forums and never pretend to be human again.

"There are parts of me that might do it. I should have killed them when they were small." She'd lost control of The Hunger years ago. It had shaped the forest beyond her home in its image, and Tillie had let it, because that meant it kept itself busy and easy to ignore.

Leilani made some noncommittal grunt. Her hand hovered at the stereo, then went back to grip the wheel. Knuckles white. Spine rigid.

"I'm not going to hurt you, Leilani."

"I hate this song," she grumbled and jabbed a button to flip to a different station. A string quartet warbled shrilly through the speakers. Leilani smacked a button and turned it off.

"I'm not the dangerous parts," Tillie started to explain, but Leilani waved her hand to silence her as she checked her mirrors.

"I'm taking this exit." The rolling hills and lush forests were unfamiliar. They were still miles from Tillie's home. "Need to stretch my legs." Leilani shivered and pulled her van into a rest stop. She turned off the car and turned toward the door. "I'll be right back," she said, then rushed out.

Tillie set some spiders down on the silk flowers to check her body. The skin was still in place, the eyes tracked perfectly with one another. The hands responded easily to the strings pulling beneath the skin.

The illusion did not matter. Leilani knew what she was, and she knew about The Hunger. Tillie should have run into the forest and made her own way back home.

Leilani returned on the passenger side of the car. She opened Tillie's door and leaned heavily on it. "I need you to explain why you think you might eat your husband."

"I don't want to."

"I got that." Her eyes were hard, but her hands were shaking. She was scared. "You told me you wouldn't hurt me."

"I won't." She said it too quickly, too harshly. The words almost tore from her throat to leap at Leilani. She was being aggressive. A monster. "I promise," she added softly. "I promise promise." Anything to keep her friend from leaving her. She didn't want to rebuild her life again. She didn't have the heart. "You can lock me in one of those storage bins if you need to be sure, but you'll have to unlatch it when you get to my house. I don't think I'll suffocate in the time it takes to get there, but I probably shouldn't test my luck."

"Stop!" shouted Leilani, to end the deluge of Tillie's pleading. She pinched the bridge of her nose and sighed. "Tillie, this day has been fucking crazy for me. I find out magic is real and you are made of spiders, and you're just sitting here, telling me there's another you out there that wants to eat your husband, and I am trying to be cool about this but it has been a lot."

"I'm sorry. I shouldn't have put this on you."

Leilani drooped. "I'm not going to hold it against you that you like... dissolved? In front of me? Obviously you didn't want to do that, and god knows I've had days I can't just pull myself together, but I do need some honesty from you." She sucked her teeth. "And I definitely don't want to shove you in a Sterlite container. That sounds cramped."

"Just the spiders. I'd leave the body in the back."

"So your solution was; I drive a tote filled with spiders and a dead body back to your house?"

"Well, it isn't a dead body. I think something has to be alive first to be dead."

"Tillie!"

The exclamation shocked Tillie into pulling her body to attention. She was performing human poorly. Leilani was going to leave her. The monster in the forest was going to eat her husband and then she would truly be alone.

"I'm sorry." She apologized without knowing what she was sorry for. Leilani frowned and she did so again. "I'm sorry." She slunk the body down in the seat and began to pull pieces of it to the back, where she could fit herself into the Sterlite and assure Leilani of her safety. "I won't hurt you. Please don't leave me here."

Leilani reached for Tillie's shoulder. "Tillie, stop!"

She stopped. The body was draped over the armrest; the head dangled off the neck.

Leilani looked over her shoulder, then moved to block the door. "Please stop looking dead. I really don't want people to think I've got a dead woman in the passenger seat of my car," she hissed through gritted teeth.

"Sorry," Tillie said again, and Leilani rolled her eyes.

"I really think you'll be happier if I'm in the bin." Her left hand began to unravel as a team made an exit. Ribbons of silken skin hung into the plastic bin and her spiders descended them in a flood.

Leilani squirmed and covered her face in her hands. "Tillie, I swear to god I will abandon this car if you do not pull yourself together right now."

Tillie reversed the flood. Skin pulled back into place as Leilani peeked through her fingers.

"Is your whole skeleton pink?"

Tillie nodded. "Yeah. I can't remember the type of filament Ivan used to print it, but yeah it's all pink. Plastic isn't dead, it's just not alive."

Leilani sighed with her entire body. "Get back in the passenger seat, you fucking weirdo. And try to keep your spiders inside your skin." She checked her phone. "We're about an hour away from your house. You are going to tell me everything about this other you that might eat your husband, and then when we get there, I'm going to drop you off. Deal?"

Tillie pulled herself back into the seat. "Of course. I'll tell you anything. Everything." She felt a phantom pressure in her throat. A lump of nerves that never existed in this body. This was a concession from Leilani. A last bit of courtesy before leaving her forever. "Thank you."

Leilani stretched and got into the driver seat. She hunched over the wheel and grumbled about a faulty starter as the car sputtered back to life.

"You don't have to send me fringe," said Tillie

Leilani stared suspiciously at her and leaned back in her chair. "Because you don't want any, or because you think you don't deserve fringe?"

"I—" the words stuck fast on her tongue. She didn't know how to answer.

Leilani wiped a bit of wet from the corner of her eye. "Everyone deserves fringe, Tillie. It doesn't matter what you're made of."

Leilani pulled out of the parking space and slowly drove them back to the on-ramp.

"My house is forty minutes from here?" asked Tillie.

"Yep," her lips popped on the sound. Her eyes were on the road as she accelerated.

"I don't really know where to start." There was so much to explain in a forty minute drive.

Leilani shrugged. She sighed. She glanced over at Tillie who was trying to make her small body even smaller in the passenger seat, and she gave her an encouraging smile. "How about, are you only friends with me for all my delicious moth illustrations?"

Tillie laughed in spite of herself. "They really are so pretty." She turned toward Leilani and returned the smile. "But moths are tastier as caterpillars."

Leilani stuck out her tongue in playful disgust. "So you eat anything, then? Not just husbands?"

"The other me did eat a husband once. You remember that neighbor girl that I babysit sometimes?" She'd shown off some of the girl's work to the rest of the chat after a few impromptu painting lessons, then printed all the praise they'd dished upon it. Ava still had them tacked on a corkboard over the desk in her room.

"With the evil ex-stepdad who once threatened to burn her house down?"

She nodded. "I caught him in the act. The other me took care of it."

"Okay. Well, that's still murder—"

"You said to be honest," said Tillie, and Leilani held up her hand.

"But! It's not the craziest thing I've accepted in the last few hours." Her fingers drummed the steering wheel and she bobbed her head in concession. "So, I guess as long as Ivan doesn't burn the house down, he's probably safe."

"He wouldn't," said Tillie. "Ivan doesn't even like candles because he's worried they might catch my cobwebs."

Leilani gestured, of course, like it was a normal thing to fear. "So there's you in my car, and there's another you that ate a guy, and there's also all the spiders that are making you... Does that mean you have two bodies or like, a million bodies?"

"I have four constructs, but if we're counting the spiders, I lost count of them at a hundred thousand."

Leilani laughed and shook her head. "A hundred thousand bodies, and you've made art your day job. God, no wonder you're so prolific."

"I don't think—" started Tillie, but Leilani stopped her protests with an arched eyebrow.

"And you're always chiming in to help on the group chat, and you helped Naomi get into that show last year..."

"She got in on her own, I just helped make some connections..."

"... and I thought it was just that you didn't sleep!"

"I do sleep, but we do it in shifts so there's always a part of me that's active."

Leilani snorted. She looked sidelong at Tillie, up and down, then returned her attention to the road. "That's cool. You're cool."

The spiders in her lungs tittered with excitement, and she pulled a shiver across her shoulders. She could not remember if, in her previous life, she ever felt so comfortable in the presence of someone who was not Ivan. She was certain she must have had friends, but such certainty only existed empirically.

It was odd, how easy it was to speak once the dam had opened, and when Leilani asked gently, a few more miles behind them, if Tillie was scared of her other self, Tillie found it a relief to answer. "Yes."

❖ ❖ ❖

When it was young, when it still dwelled within the horde that called itself Tillie, The Hunger had brushed its teeth against Ivan's soft skin and wondered how much he would give of himself if asked. The thought began a revolt, and the spiders that remembered their nature, that animal need to kill and eat, were forced out of Tillie Wright.

They had wandered into the forest; a hated and nameless thing that found unity in hunger. They became It. And it found somebody's dog.

The dog had sniffed at the spiders, curious about the unified swarm. It sniffed at them, opened its mouth to close curious teeth around fragile spider bodies. The spiders climbed up its jaw and bit venom into the dog's face. It yipped and struggled and spiders were crushed in the fight, but the swarm was swift. It bit all down the spine, sunk venom there. The dog thrashed and twisted to fight against the swarm, but it could not, and the spiders watched the dog die while they feasted on its flesh.

When the softer morsels were stripped away, The Hunger dragged the dog's bones deep into the forest and set them aside. A bloody collar was still around its neck.

Someone had loved the dog, and in spite of its nature, someone had loved The Hunger once, too. The dog was not food like the boxes of crickets or an errant bird caught in a web. It would be missed, and that sentiment called for some ceremony.

The Hunger buried the collar, but the bones sang to it. The Hunger was just as much an artist as the woman who cast it aside, and so it listened to the bones, and it began to build.

※ ※ ※

The Hunger ate dogs and rabbits and deer and birds and fish. It hunted elk and bear when they dared venture near her forest. It collected the largest ribcages of its prey and lashed them together in descending order, the open broken mouths of the cages pointed toward the sky. It used those bones to rig countless arms and hands, many-jointed, many-fingered, made from the bones of the many animals it devoured, and when it walked through the forest like a centipede held aloft on spider legs, the force of its movement perforated the ground and shook the trees.

The Hunger's body had no head. A hundred animal jaws crowned the face of its body, lashed together in interlocking radials. The teeth pointed outward, a crown for a queen. There was nothing left living in the forest to challenge The Hunger's sovereignty.

And it felt good to reign. The forest would die without The Hunger's work, pollinating and scattering seed and turning over the mulch of the earth. The forest kept on under its care, and that felt like something akin to love.

※ ※ ※

Mavis was caught in The Hunger's web. She tore at it with abandon, but The Hunger was close, and its spiders strung more strands than she could tear away. Her arms were slowing. Her feet were stopped. Her mouth was drawn tight, a thin line. Her eyes were hollow and bruised.

The Hunger had expected a witch. Mavis was a giant in The Hunger's memory, but the woman who panicked and struggled against the web was so very very small.

Mavis turned as The Hunger pushed trees aside. She made a pathetic little squeak as The Hunger's limbs fell in a cage around her. It picked her up in a hand built from the long tibias of elk and dropped her into the hollow cavity it made of a hundred broken ribs.

"Tillie?" Mavis's hands pressed against the webbing that made this cavity soft. It was a basket to carry prey, to carry a feast as The Hunger propelled its massive body through the forest. A spider bit Mavis as she touched it, and she pulled her arms tight against her chest.

"Tillie, how can you live like this?"

The Hunger wanted so badly to eat her. It would be much easier to eat her and make her disappear. It could do it now. The taste of Mavis's blood filtered through the network of spiders and as it disseminated, passing down the chain, the memory of it grew sweeter.

Mavis inspected the hand that The Hunger bit. Spots of blood welled up from her palm. She curled into a ball and began to cry. Her abject refusal to fight soured the taste of her blood.

Faces formed between ribs, mouths and soft bark teeth stretched between arm and body. Some of The Hunger's hands turned inward to pry Mavis open, to force her to see. The hands were not gentle as they hoisted her. They were tipped in wolves teeth made to hunt and tear. They pulled her arms and legs away and twisted her around until Mavis couldn't help but see the monster that held her. Mouths opened wherever mouths could be sewn and they all screamed in a singular roar.

"Fight BACK."

Mavis closed her eyes and turned her head, leaving her neck exposed and fragile. Everything about her was so fragile. Her mouth opened and tears fell in, garbling her words as she sobbed. "Please let me find him before you kill me."

It was a reasonable request; to say goodbye. And while The Hunger may have hated Mavis, it knew that it could not have existed without her. It did feel some meager gratitude to the witch. Enough to honor a final request. The Hunger dropped Mavis back into the basket of bone and web, and turned its senses toward the forest. It would find her feathered son.

Nothing could move within the forest without drawing its eyes.

❈ ❈ ❈

Ivan carried the upper half of a murdered man in his arms, while Tillie rode silently within the bones. She stroked his shoulder in thanks and apology and reverence, both with borrowed hands and her own claws. She had stopped apologizing aloud to him when he threatened to drop her if she repeated the word "sorry" one more time.

Ivan was tired. His feet hurt, and the body in his arms was heavy. He followed where it directed him, through sopping leaves and over marshy ground. His pants were wet up to his knees, and his sneakers were caked in mud. They were following The Hunger.

Tillie wished she could carry him.

The Hunger could have carried him as easily as carrying a kitten. All its cantilevered arms and reinforced hands, the way it walked so steadily, never fewer than three points of contact on the ground. She envied its freedom. It was not afraid to leave the confines of a human shape. While she scuttled her torso about the house and propped it wherever she might need her voice, The Hunger crafted as many hands as it desired to carry it through the forest.

She could have built legs for herself, tipped the end in hands with steady claws, enough of them that she would never fall. But it would mean bringing The Hunger's kills inside the home, and explaining where she found all those bones.

"You don't have to carry me," she whispered. "We could leave the body here and I can walk underfoot."

"I'd miss your voice," said Ivan.

They hadn't spoken for a long while. She'd stopped when he asked her to stop saying sorry.

He hitched the torso higher on his hip and adjusted the arms. She tightened their grip around his shoulders.

"I miss you," he said.

"The dead me?"

His eyebrow furrowed. "You're not dead."

"The human one."

"You're still human." He set her on the ground, propping her against a tree and leaned back, arms in the air. His sweater pulled up, exposing his fleshy, hairy stomach. His back popped loudly, and he sighed. "Your spirit is human. I don't care about anything else."

"I miss her."

He pursed his lips, then slowly lowered to sit on the ground across from the body, giving her plenty of time to scatter away from where he sat.

"Your butt will get wet."

He shrugged. "I'll dry." He brought his hand up to where Eyeball sat on his shoulder. She climbed onto his palm, and he brought her down to speak eye to eye. "How long have you missed her?"

The body wheezed behind the spider in his hand, something almost like a cry. "I miss how easy it was."

"It was never easy. It was easier, maybe, but never easy."

"Because I'm difficult."

"Everyone is difficult, honey. It comes with being human. But you are worth some difficulties. And I hope you think I'm worth it, too."

"Ivan. Of course. You're not... when have you ever been difficult?"

"Honey." He laughed and held her up and pressed a gentle kiss to her thorax. "You have been shut in for too long if you think I'm a cakewalk."

"I honestly don't know what you're talking about."

"Nothing? I've never annoyed you even once?"

Her spiders chittered in the body and clacked their mandibles together. "Nothing," she lied, because he never finished the dishes he started, or remembered to sweep after cooking, and these complaints were so small that they felt like nothing in the face of all the good he did for her.

He sighed. "Well, that just tells me you need to spend more time with other people."

As the words left his tongue, his face fell, and the same thought jolted through them both. They shouted her name in unison.

"E. Leilani Liu!"

The spider in his hands jumped to the ground and ran for the body. "I fell apart! What if I'm a cloud of spiders? What if she sees?"

"Fuck!" Ivan pulled his phone from his back pocket. "Oh, fuck, it's been on silent. She's been trying to call me."

"No no no no no she's going to freak out!"

"It's okay. It'll be okay. Shit! Service sucks here. Can I..." He got up, marched around the forest, waving his hand in the air trying to catch a signal. "Okay, I think I got it..." The phone rang, and Tillie cinched her body up the tree to keep her head level with his. "Oh my god it went through!"

❖ ❖ ❖

The Artist unlocked the door to her house. Leilani stood behind her, idly taking in the bland grey siding, the pollen dusted chair on the porch. There were cobwebs in every corner, and a wince echoed across every single spider in her body. Tillie bit back the urge to apologize, because Leilani had forbidden her from saying "sorry" after their conversation in the car steered back to The Hunger. Tillie pushed the door open, then wheeled herself inside and spun around to beckon Leilani to follow.

"Cute place," said Leilani. She nodded at the crowded wall of pictures. The discordant frames were puzzle-pieced so closely that the yellow wall was barely visible, seen only in the margins between a slew of mediums and styles. Leilani recognized the paintings immediately; pieces from all the friends at their retreat, and a few that could not make it, but had promised to come if they did it again. "You should share this wall with the group chat. I think everyone would love to see us all hanging together."

Tillie shrugged. "I should clean first." The frames were dusty. Webs hung down from the ceiling in pale sheets, like Halloween decor. "Looks like a goddamn haunted house in here."

Leilani chuckled. "Well, if I understand it correctly, you're basically a ghost, right? Haunting a hundred thousand spiders?"

Tillie nodded.

"I don't think they'd mind. I think Andrew, you know Naomi's partner? He cuts together short films out of abandoned home videos and uploads them as ghost stories. He'd probably be—"

"Please don't tell anyone," she whispered, in a voice so soft it barely left the threads of her vocal chords.

"Sorry." Leilani bit her lip. "We were joking in the car, but I guess I never asked... does it bother you to be like this? You said used to be afraid of spiders."

The Artist pressed a sigh out of her lips. She didn't have another way of being. "I don't hate it, but I don't want to be a spectacle." Spiders abandoned her arms and torso to run out through the feet, leaving in a flood of brown specks so dark they looked like pepper floating across the ground. "And I don't want to scare anyone else away."

The spiders dispersed throughout the house. It was too still. There was no breathing thing within it to move any strands of web. No soft and steady thrum of his heartbeat. Her focus flitted through a thousand eyes as she searched her entire house.

There was a cocoon of spidersilk laying in the sunroom. It was human sized, but too small for Ivan. Her good scissors were laying on the ground beside it, neat snips having let whatever she'd captured out. A few of her crushed bodies smeared the floor. She must have left in a hurry, to leave without giving her dead the dignity of being eaten and brought back into the fold.

A regiment split to scrape up the remains, devour them, while the rest of her continued through the house.

She found her other self crumpled on the couch. The rainbow blanket sat oddly over her skeleton.

"Oh," she said in the foyer.

Leilani blanched. "What?"

"It's probably fine."

"That's not very reassuring while I'm watching your..." She hesitated, eyes ghosting over the flood of tiny spiders that were still falling from Tillie's skirt. "...bits scuttle away from your plastic feet."

"I found my body in the den." Hundreds of claws gripped the edge of the blanket that covered it like a shroud and began to pull it away from the bones.

"How do we feel about that?" Leilani asked slowly. "Is it The Hunger?" Her voice squeaked. She was scared.

Tillie was scaring her, and she could not stop scaring her, because her spiders were in shock and her mind was split and she said "Something crushed my sternum" because putting words to it made a little more sense of the mangled jagged bones of her skeleton. The bones were splintered. Pieces of them were left tangled in the cobweb batting she used to fill out her middle. "It's broken." She pulled at strands inside the plastic body, plucking aimlessly behind the eyes. "I don't know how to fix that." She kept plucking at the face, as if a hidden strand could manifest tears. "I can't fix it."

The Artist's body slumped forward as the spiders in her lungs scattered down to move the chair forward through her house. She had another sternum, another set of ribs. They weren't correct. They were pink and the material was oily on her claws and new and it did not cling to web with the same grace as bone, but she couldn't leave her bones lying broken and forgotten and alone.

Leilani yelped as the body fell over in the wheelchair and vaguely, a part of Tillie knew she should have apologized for upsetting her. Surely this was the end. Leilani was already afraid. But Leilani steeled herself and ducked beneath the cobwebs and ran after the wheelchair. "Can I help? Please. I want to help."

Spiders flooded back into the body's torso. They set her upright and wrenched at the strands for speech. "It doesn't look like The Hunger's work." She was pulling too hard. The voice sounded rough and mean and she hated to sound mean when Leilani had already forgiven so much. Spiders scrabbled at one another, fought until only the most delicate claws were operating her strands and she smoothed her voice to explain. "It may resent me, but it would never break our bones."

There were popcorn kernels scattered on the ground. The heavy bowl was set at the foot of the couch, just beneath where her empty body was propped against the pillows. It was the same size as the cavity shattered into the ribs

Leilani now stood frozen over the artist's shoulder. She stared at the body on the couch. The exposed bone; white and clean and broken.

"I should have warned you." Tillie bit at the idea of sorry and stuffed it back down into her lungs. "That's the dead body. That's the body that was living, but something broke her. The popcorn bowl."

"Where is Ivan?" Leilani asked, softly.

"I don't taste blood. Whatever broke my ribs didn't come for him." Tillie tore at the mask of her face from behind, furious that she could not cry, and determined to leave tracks of something to relieve some pressure. "I think I'm scared."

"Don't fall apart on me, okay? Keep it together, Tillie. You can be scared, but you have to keep yourself together."

"I don't want to be scared."

Leilani huffed and gave her a tight smile. "We can be scared together, okay?"

"Are you afraid of me?"

"I'm just afraid of what happened." She gestured to the broken body on the couch, and Tillie flinched that the thing looked so horribly dead. Its face hung slack, and only its lack of blood kept the open cave of its chest from gore. "Obviously something scary happened here. Just because you're the one haunting the house, it doesn't mean you can't be scared."

The spiders behind her mask stopped snipping and Tillie coughed a sad little laugh out of her lungs.

Leilani's phone buzzed. She reached for it. Paused. Bit her lip. "Should I?" she said, then sighed and picked it up anyway. "Oh shit it's Ivan!"

Tillie cinched the torso upright and Leilani startled, dropping the phone.

"Fuck! Answer it answer it!" shouted Leilani.

"I can't!" Tillie scrabbled for it; several spiders held it aloft to get it back into Leilani's hands.

Leilani answered, and Ivan shouted through the phone: "Everything is normal!"

"Ivan? Ivan, no, this is not normal. Nothing is normal. Who calls like this? What the fuck, man? Do you want to talk to your wife?"

"She's—" He spoke to someone behind him, then the voice returned to the phone. "You have a Tillie there, too?"

"Can you put it on video?" asked Tillie.

Leilani turned the phone around and knelt on the floor, holding it out for Tillie to see. Ivan's heavily pixelated face was too close to the camera. His strained voice peaked the sound on the phone. "Tillie! You're still you!"

Tillie heard her own voice laugh behind him, and Ivan turned away from the phone. "Right? I thought you said you couldn't feel her."

Another version of her pushed her way onto the screen. "I couldn't, but apparently she's fine!" This Tillie was in the backup body. Its broad chest and mossy bones looked wretched next to Ivan, but he didn't even glance aside as it shoved its eyeless face next to his.

He shouldn't be in the forest. He shouldn't know about the dead man, and the body she made of his bones. He needed to leave.

The horrible corpse pulled its mask into a grin and addressed her. "How did you get home?"

"I drove her," said Leilani.

"Why are you in the forest?" asked The Artist.

"We're chasing—" The sound on the phone fuzzed out and cut away, and the picture fractured into pixels. Tillie's spiders caught their breath, and then the sound crackled and came back to life. "…The Hunger."

Tillie seized the phone. "He knows?"

"I know, Tillie," said Ivan. "You told me."

The Artist felt a horror creep through all her spiders, and she took a deep breath to give them something to focus on. He knew, and he was still next to her, smiling gently through the phone.

"What happened? Did The Hunger break our ribs?"

The other her shook her head. "It was Mavis."

Her bodies writhed with fury. "Mavis came back just to *break my ribs?* I haven't seen her in years. Why would she do that?"

"The witch?" Leilani asked softly.

"Yes." She pulled her jaw to click the plastic teeth twice, savoring the strength in her bite. "I could fucking kill her."

"We might—" the phone fuzzed into static again.

The artist gripped the misbehaving thing in two hands and shook it, as if she could rattle a signal into submission.

"Please don't break my phone," said Leilani softly, and Tillie remembered she was still here. And helping. And while Tillie could not shatter Leilani's phone in her hands, she was not being a very good borrower.

The green haze of pixels arranged themselves into a clear picture of the practice body's face. It's bright river-rock eyes furrowed in concern, amid a backdrop of blue sky. "Can you hear me?"

"Yes!"

"Okay! Good! I mean, not all the way good. Ivan and I are in the forest and The Hunger is going to eat Mavis unless we can find her first."

"Where is The Hunger?"

"I don't—" The phone slipped away from the other Tillie's face, then jumbled around in her graceless hands until it came to rest pointed outward toward the canopy of the forest. "Do you see that?" A wood-boned finger pointed out toward a line of trees that seemed to be parting like a river. "Shit. I should have climbed a tree hours ago."

"Is that The Hunger?" Tillie peered at the screen with a dozen eyes, but the picture wasn't clear.

"Yes. By the grove of bluebirds, moving toward The Lanterns."

Ivan shouted up from below, his voice distant. "What the fuck is "The Lanterns?'"

Tillie sighed. "Tell Ivan we love him?"

Her own face smiled back at her through the phone. A little broader than it ought to be, the eyes a strange slate gray, but the pull of the smile was the same, and the ill-fitting bones were not so hideous when she smiled. "Of course."

The other her reached for the phone to hang up, and Tillie blurted "I miss you," before she could stop herself from saying so.

The other her smirked. "I love you, too."

The phone went dark. Tillie held it out for Leilani, thankful that any blood that might have reddened her face in a blush had dried long ago. "I don't know why I said that."

Leilani shrugged. "It's cute. I don't know. If I had a copy of myself the first thing I'd do is probably give her a hug. Maybe some words of validation."

"Do you want a hug?" asked Tillie.

"I am being very brave," confessed Leilani. "I think I've earned one."

Tillie offered her arms, and Leilani crouched into them. "Thank you for being brave. I am so sorry you had to see all of... well. Everything."

Leilani pulled out Ivan's kitchen chair to sit across from her. "I think you've had a worse day. I don't have an estranged sister breaking my ribs."

"I should go find Mavis before the other me—the *other* other me—eats her."

"You should. But..." Leilani looked over at the skeleton on the couch. The mask on its face was sagging, the jaw slung open. Even covered, it was clearly a desiccated corpse, the shattered ribs making peaks in the blanket over its chest. It was a horrible sight. "You know, my partner Bree has done some work with animal bones. When she was in college she articulated some skeletons for a museum. Had to do some repairs on a few of them, too. She's talked about wanting to get back into it."

"There's no disguising a human ribcage. She'll know what it is immediately."

Leilani nodded. She reached across the table. "So we'll tell her why you need human ribs repaired. I'm sure she won't mind. Bree loves creepy shit."

Tillie stared at the offered hand. "I should... I should go. I don't want to kill my sister." Her spiders were already evacuating. The team in her shoulders stopped to untie the green scarf from her neck and carry it over to Leilani's hand, but Leilani pushed it back toward her.

"You can keep that for the rest of the week. I'm driving by here anyway when the retreat is over. Maybe we can get…" she bit her lip. "Wait. You don't drink coffee." She shook her head. "Oh my god I've seen those pictures of spiderwebs from caffeinated spiders, that makes so much sense now."

Tillie laughed. "It doesn't go well."

"We don't need drinks. Maybe we can just visit and talk about our plans for next year's retreat."

"You still want me?"

Leilani reached over the spiders holding her scarf to give Tillie a gentle pat on her shoulder. "Do you know how many texts I've been answering from people asking if you're okay? Not even just folks at the retreat, everyone on the message board is worrying about you. You're a pillar of the community, friend." She winked. "Granted, a pillar of spiders, but I'm going to keep that between us."

"How are you so cool?"

Leilani barked a laugh. "I'm actually freaking out one hundred percent of the time. I'm not saying I'm 100% fine to learn that you're secretly made of spiders and magic is real, but it's kind of nice that the insane thing is happening outside my head, instead of me just making up things to be scared about."

"That sounds really hard."

She smiled. "We've all got our struggles. I'll see you Monday, okay? If I leave now I can get back to the retreat in time to help with dinner."

"Monday," said Tillie, and waved with the last of the spiders in her wrists as Leilani jogged out the door.

🕷 🕷 🕷

The Hunger crashed through the forest with Mavis caged inside its ribs. It was wandering aimlessly, touching every strand of web it crossed, seeking any sign of Mavis's son through its vibration, but the bird remained hidden.

Mavis did not appreciate her position as The Hunger's temporary heart. She stopped sobbing at least, but her the tang of fear laced through her sweat, and her flesh was salted with tears.

She straightened her tatty sweater and rode within the ribs like a queen in a palanquin. The Hunger admired her. Even as it marched her to her death, the iron in Mavis's spine would not bend.

It wondered if her son knew of his mother's strength. If the little bird could even recognize it, for all his fluttering and screeching.

It was a terrible thing to be a bird. There was no place in the world that was truly safe for a single bird. Just as there was no place safe for a single spider. The Hunger had numbers. It had banded together and remade the forest until The Hunger was the only thing in it, but the boy was small and alone.

It was cruelty.

Mouths opened across the basket of bone and web where Mavis was caged. Disparate voices coalesced into a singular question. "Why did you make him a bird?"

Mavis glared at the nearest mouth. "You're talking to me now?"

"You should have made him something bigger. Birds die so easily."

"You would know something about that, wouldn't you."

"I won't eat your bird." The mouths tipped upward into cruel smiles.

Mavis twitched with rage. "I didn't make him anything. He was born that way. A curse. He's only human when he's sleeping and I've been trying to fix it—"

The Hunger tasted an absence within Mavis and all the mouths pulled into a sneer. "You're not a witch anymore," it hissed in a twisted delight.

The Hunger stopped its thundering procession and turned a few arms inward to better inspect its sister. Mavis pulled away, but a massive hand built of deer legs pinned her in place while spiders scuttled up to taste her sweat for any lingering magic.

"What happened?"

Her fingers and palms were pocked and scarred, but long healed. It must have been years since she last embroidered a spell into her skin.

"You." Mavis spat the word, and the hand withdrew.

The mouths growled "No" in unison, but The Hunger was not so certain. How many years had it been since that odd afternoon, when suddenly every spider felt alight with inspiration? Their connection stronger than before, the masks and bodies that worked with perfect unity to perfect her masquerade. It was no longer a puppet, but a gestalt. A creature in its own right.

Tillie thought it was practice, but there was something more. Even Ivan could forget at times what she was, because she wore her mask so well.

"No?" Mavis kicked at the massive hand and hissed at the pain when it was stronger than her foot. "You think you're this disgusting thing without magic?"

"You think I stole it."

"You didn't steal it. I gave it away. And it went to you." She seethed. "Because we're linked. You might not have blood anymore but the magic knows our bones are the same." She glared at the cage of bone around her. "And this is what you do with it."

"I didn't choose to be a monster."

"Bullshit. I saw you at the house. You looked human. You think you don't have magic, but you can look like whatever you want. And you chose this hulking, disgusting—"

"I am what you made me!"

"You made yourself!" Mavis screeched and tore at the cobwebs surrounding her. "You wound yourself up in this crazy idea that a spider was eating your heart, and by the time I got there you'd made it true."

"I'm not a witch," The Hunger's voices thundered around her.

"I don't care what you call yourself, Tillie. Magic sticks to you. I did what I could to fix it, but *this* is what you made of it." Mavis bared her teeth at the cage of bone, at the spiders inhabiting it. "You wanted this. Why?"

"Why are you calling me Tillie?" The body in the house had not been given the same courtesy. Mavis called it 'creature,' and 'monster,' and 'thing."

Mavis ceased her rending and dropped sheets of spiderweb to the floor. She choked, and bit away tears as she flexed her fists. "Because you sound like her." Her voice cracked and she rubbed roughly at her eyes. "Because you sound like my bratty little sister and I miss her. Why did you break yourself apart, Tillie?"

The Hunger closed its mouths. The venom stopped on its teeth. It's appetite was gone. "Bratty?"

"I wasn't ready to take care of you when mom died. Of course I thought you were a brat. I was just a stupid kid. I was barely out of the house and suddenly I had a ten year old to take care of."

The Hunger retracted its press of mouths to give Mavis a bit more space. "I wasn't easy," admitted The Hunger. It remembered so little of the time before, but it knew of their fights. How hard Mavis was to please, and how Tillie stopped trying.

"Neither was I," said Mavis. "And I'm just so tired of everyone dying around me."

"I'm still here."

"Are you?"

She was. The Hunger was only another mask. And beneath it, the lost parts of Tillie weren't angry anymore. All she could feel was sorrow.

"I'm sorry, Mavis."

"Don't." The word ripped from her lungs to pounce with teeth and claws. Mavis stood on shaking legs, her fingers dug into web and bone to steady her. "I can't hear another apology from you. You died and then I left you because I was scared and I didn't know... I didn't know it was still you."

"I hated you for leaving," said Tillie.

"I hated myself."

Tillie conferred within herself, within The Hunger. She knew self-hatred. It was what made her into this. The feeling seemed so small, now that it was named.

"You had a kid."

Mavis nodded. "I love him."

Tillie plucked the strings of her arms and pulled the great body of The Hunger to stand. "And you can't find him."

Mavis choked. "I wish I had my magic back. I wish I had Mackenzie."

Tillie sorted through her manufactured hands until she found a softer one, made for delicate work. It had too many fingers, and the moss that padded its palm was beginning to shed, but it was the best she could do in this body. She pushed it through the web that caged Mavis in her ribs and laid it gently on her shoulder. "Maybe I can help?"

Mavis blinked away tears and set her jaw tight. "How," she breathed.

"I don't know how to cast a spell, but you do. Tell me how to find him."

※ ※ ※

Mavis worked best with blood. Her own blood no longer carried magic, but it was connected to Freddie, and the spidersilk that surrounded her was choked with it. Tillie's spirit could not have survived within the spiders without magic binding them together. Mavis only wished that it manifested in something less horrific. But, when Mavis had worked her magic into her sister to give her more time, she had been working with a corpse.

"How bad would it be for you to bite me? Are you poisonous?"

"Venomous," corrected Tillie in a hundred voices. "But not terribly so. The venom liquifies bugs, not people."

Mavis pulled a face and Tillie shook out several hands in frustration.

"Oh, like that's the worst thing you've heard today."

The magic had been a curse when Mavis held it. She saw everything. All the bright and singing threads of connection through the world. They hovered around her, loud and brittle and crowding toward her hands, where a single touch could tangle them and make things happen that should not.

She ran from it. She made her world small, spoke to no one, saw nothing, until she met Mackenzie. A fellow witch who had been looking for an out.

"I need you to draw blood. Enough to coat a strand of thread about..." Mavis bit her lip considering, then held out her arms. "Three feet long."

"Can I take it from your wrist?"

Mavis nodded. A spider with a body the size of her hand walked out of the wall of web and crawled onto her arm. Mavis closed her eyes and held her arm as far from herself as she could, her stomach roiling in revulsion.

Her partner was dead. Her son was a bird. Her sister was a monster. Everything turned wrong around her, with magic or without. She was cursed at her core, and she could not escape it.

And even now, with Tillie beneath Mavis's feet, helping to work a spell, she was trapped. She could not kill the sister that was helping her in order to save her son.

This spell they would work together would only find him. She had no way to dispel his curse. She would devote her life to caring for her bird in a palace of a cage, and only see her son while he was sleeping. She would never know the person he could be.

And if Mavis outlived him, because swallows do not live for very long, she would let her sister eat her. Maybe Tillie could make something of her useless bones.

"Why are you crying? Did the bite hurt that bad?" Tillie's voices, the concert of them, were quieter. A moss padded hand with too many fingers held Mavis's wrist steady for the spider that had already bit her arm.

Mavis hadn't even felt it.

"It didn't hurt," she said in a hoarse whisper. She watched the massive spider as it drew a strand of silk over the bite. Every few inches, it would stop to push at the wound with its claws and coax more blood to the surface.

"Please don't squash that one, Mavis. It's one of my oldest."

"I—" she shook her head. "I wouldn't."

The spider bobbed its head at her, then continued to pull a strand of silk through her blood.

"Is this enough?" asked Tillie.

"Yes." Mavis sighed. "You don't have a needle with you?" Along with blood, Mavis had worked with embroidery. There was a ritual inherent to the craft—a method of intention—that could align thought with reality, and coax it into being. When she hadn't been able to control the magic around her, she'd turned that embroidery on herself, and stitched spells into her own skin.

"I can make one," said Tillie. A moment later, a bone white needle rose from the floor of the cage into the spider's claw, and it laid the thing in Mavis's hand. "Will this work?"

Mavis nodded. She threaded the blood soaked silk through the needle.

"Does it have to be on skin?" asked Tillie. "I don't have any left." The many mouths pulled taut in embarrassed smiles. "Sorry."

"I hope not." Mavis chose a patch of woven spidersilk that looked smoother than the rest, closer to the crown of jaws. She would have preferred to stitch her spell near the eyes, but for all the construct's mouths, it had no head to speak of.

Mavis was not an artist. Not like Tillie. Her stitches were wobbly and imprecise. When she embroidered her skin, the practice was more important than the outcome. It was difficult to establish any true skill when the canvas was always moving, and every stitch could sting. But it made her fast, and within minutes, she had a recognizable compass rose stitched into the construct, and a little letter F marked at north.

"Can you feel him?" asked Mavis. She pulled back from where she'd crouched over her embroidery and stretched. It had been a few years since she had to stitch in a strange position. The spider that bit her had never left her side, and it looked up at her as she flexed some feeling back into her fingers, its head tilted slightly as it lifted itself higher on its legs.

"I didn't feel the needle. It doesn't feel like anything," said the voices of her sister.

Mavis shuddered. There was no getting used to the voices, all like Tillie, but filtered through the wrong materials, wrong sizes, wrong shapes. That body Mavis met inside the house sounded like the Tillie she'd left ten years ago. This one was wrong, but it felt more true.

"Mavis? The magic isn't working. Did I do something wrong?"

"I think it needs to hurt," said Mavis. "It always hurt when I did it."

The spider poked at the compass rose stitched in silk and blood. The blood on the strand was already wicked away by the surrounding silk. Any real distinction between stitch and web was nearly lost outside of the punctures left by the needle, and Tillie suspected that it would take a spider's eye to see them.

"I don't really have nerves that hurt like yours do." She felt loss when her spiders died, but pain was a distant memory. "What if I eat it?"

Mavis shrugged. "Worth a shot?"

She unpicked the embroidery from where Mavis had stitched it, bundling blood and silk alike to stuff inside her mouth. The blood tasted like any other blood. The silk like silk, but as she ingested it, and brought it back into this miniscule part of her fold to be used again, a vibration wobbled at the furthest edge of her perception.

A bird was caught in her web. Far away, toward The Lanterns, where The Hunger collected bone and glass and sea trash and decorated the trees with every beautiful thing that it could not find a place for within its body.

"I know where he is," said Tillie. Her spiders took their stations throughout the mighty body of The Hunger and raised it to stand on its hundred arms. Mavis tipped over in the cage of bone and twisted horribly to keep herself from squashing the spider that sat beside her. That many-fingered hand pushed through again and helped her to stand, then locked in place to brace her as the body lumbered through the forest.

"Is he okay?" Mavis asked through gasping breath, her knuckles white where she clenched onto the offered hand.

"He's alive," said Tillie. Now that she could sense him, she could feel the panicked thrashing, the broken webs. He had been in this state for hours, and she did not know how long a bird could panic before his heart might burst. "We need to hurry." The spiders abandoned the mouths to aid their fellows at the arms. She needed to run.

※ ※ ※

Ivan was running for The Lanterns. The practice body was lashed to his back with straps of woven spidersilk, and he followed a stream of Tillie's spiders as they rushed along the ground, through the trees, a river of scuttling legs and bobbing striped bodies.

She explained The Lanterns as they ran. The Hunger made its home inside the forest, and portioned it into vast and nebulous rooms. The practice body was kept like a prize doll in The Throne Room. Small prey was reassembled with spidersilk pelts and fishbone whiskers, squirrels and rats and mice, and placed into The Menagerie. The Hunger had a special fondness for rabbits, and when it caught them, it reserved their skeletons for a growing collection in a massive hollow stump it called The Warren.

Beyond that, at the farthest reaches of its territory, The Hunger built its lanterns out of sea trash and other treasures stolen from the neighbors' refuse. It strung them in the trees to collect the light. The effect lasted for only a moment in the evening, when the sun dipped below the haze of web that diffused any light that might pierce the forest's canopy, but when the light caught the shards of glass and mirror and shiny things The Hunger had built into the center of all its lanterns, it lit the forest in a hundred tiny suns.

"I thought The Hunger was separate from you."

"Mostly," wheezed the body strapped to his back. "But I get updates sometimes. It shares art projects with me, when it's near the house."

He grunted and hiked the body higher on his back.

"I don't even hear it anymore. Your discards are fucking fast."

Shame rippled across all her bodies to hear him call them discards.

"What if we're too late?" asked Ivan.

"I can't think about that."

"If it kills your sister and joins with you—"

"I can't think about that, Ivan!" She didn't mean to shout at him. She should never shout at him. He deserved better than that.

"Then we'll make it work!" he shouted back. "We'll make it work." He bit his lip. He kept moving, but his pace slowed. He was tiring, because he was not made for running through a forest. "Whatever this thing is, obviously it's still part of you. It—it likes beautiful things. It can't be all bad. Whatever happens, Tillie, I love you."

"I don't want you to be afraid of me."

"It's a little late for that." The words were choked out through tears. But he laughed through them, shook his head, and smiled. "But we're going to make that work, too."

❊ ❊ ❊

The Lanterns were dim when The Hunger's body came to a halt beneath them. Tillie laid its bones down at the foot of the tree where Freddie was caught. A few hundred spiders chewed a door for her sister at the bottom of the rib cage, and the gentle, many-fingered hand helped Mavis step out of the cage.

Mavis could not see her son from the ground. Neither could Tillie, but she could feel him struggling against her web, high in the tree. He felt small. A frantic, winged thing. His beak could easily crush a single spider, but she had numbers, and he was already pinned.

"He'll stay a bird while he's awake?" she asked Mavis. She could carry a bird down from the tree tops. A boy would be more difficult, and the tenor of his fear was driving him dangerously close to fainting.

"He will." She looked curiously at The Hunger, searching for a face to address. "Why?"

"Nothing," she murmured across all her mouths, then abandoned them to swarm the bulk of her self up the tree. Her largest spiders lead the way. Smaller ones wove their webs into twine and then rope and then nets to hold the bird tight and keep him from plucking out her legs while she carried him down. The elder spiders were the only ones strong enough to hold him, and she signaled three of her largest to take the net and capture him from behind.

The bird was shaking. His foot was twisted so far that it looked broken, but he did not fight like a broken thing would. He was still. His black eyes centered on the small spider nearest to him. His beak opened, tongue flicked against the air, tasting her on the wind.

She could see the hunger in him. It was a long flight from the house to The Lanterns. He'd struggled for hours. He was starving. And small. And surrounded by hundreds of reaching claws that could pierce through his feathers and pull him apart. She understood the animal fear, and how dangerous he could be.

She steadied herself across the spiders. Individually, they knew to fear his sharp beak, his darting tongue. It was natural for a bird to eat a spider and for a spider to fear death.

And it was natural for a woman to love her family. She did love him. Intellectually, she had to, because she loved the idea of him even though she had never met him before today, did not know of his existence, and now barely knew the sister who waited far below, her breath shallow and fearful and still unable to fully trust the monster that surrounded her son.

A small spider edged closer to him. She needed to free his twisted foot from the web and ensure she did not injure it further.

Freddie snatched it up, and swallowed it whole.

Fear rippled across the spiders surrounding him, and she had nowhere to send it. The Hunger was all of her. All of its fear and anger and hurt was mixed together and fighting to be heard. It demanded retribution for the eaten spider. It was owed a life.

A spider reared over the bird, fangs bared, claws poised to strike.

She plunged a leg through the back of the spider's head and severed it from its body. That leg was quickly torn away as several spiders pulled it apart. The spiders turned on one another, and Tillie went to war with her self.

Far below, Mavis stared up into the canopy, while a contingent of Tillie stood ready within the mouth nearest her.

"What's taking so long?"

"He ate a spider."

"You have millions."

"And they all want to live."

"Tillie, if you eat him, I swear—"

A many jointed hand made from wolf tibia and tipped in teeth landed gently on Mavis's shoulder. "Please. I'm concentrating."

Mavis glared at her, but she remained silent.

The culling was violent. Claws tore deep into soft joints to rend them apart. Eyes were pierced, legs were ripped away. Bodies fell from the trees and rained gore below. The bird froze in place, too terrified to cry out.

This was all going wrong. What a terrible first impression. She wanted to be a good auntie. She wanted him to love her.

The thought rippled through her, that desire to be loved, and she forced herself to follow that idea.

Freddie was her nephew. Freddie had eaten a spider, but a single spider was a sorry meal for a growing boy. There was food all around him now, bodies flying apart as her spiders fought for retribution or for mercy or simply because they were angry and something needed to hurt. And she hadn't offered him any of it. Tillie gathered the bodies she had killed and pushed them towards the little bird, begging for his forgiveness, that he might learn to love her.

The boy's head cocked, his little tongue darted out of the beak. The promise of food overrode his fear. He snapped the spiders from her outstretched claws.

He swallowed. His eyes closed in joy, and he promptly fell from the tree. She leapt to grasp at the webs that held him, but they burst as the little talon suddenly became a foot. A boy crashed down through the branches.

Mavis screamed for Freddie. Tillie pulled The Hunger's body to life and stretched it skyward, weaving and weaving to catch him. Hands over hands over hands pulled The Hunger up into the trees. Freddie broke through the first hand, and another scraped at him, and another caught his arm, another wrapped around his body, and he slowed as he fell until Tillie set him gently down on the ground.

He was boy-shaped and sized, but feathers grew from his face and head. His eyes were a beady black when he opened them and he blinked at her with an animal's understanding. Mavis fell into a hug around him, and he ignored her to lick spider guts from his fingers and snap his teeth greedily at the ones that quickly moved just beyond his reach.

Tillie gathered the remains of the violence she had enacted upon herself. Twitching spiders, broken legs, severed heads. She pushed them toward her nephew, an offering, and fell back to give him space.

He ate his fill, then fell asleep in his mother's arms.

🕷 🕷 🕷

Freddie was asleep when Ivan and Tillie found The Hunger. The massive, many-limbed body made of bone and silk was coiled around Mavis like a sleeping cat. She in turn was curled around a small sleeping child, her arms and legs so tight they seemed frozen that way.

The Hunger did not move as they approached. Ivan stopped far from its reach and let Tillie's body slip from his back and slump onto the forest floor. "What do we do now?" he asked softly.

"I don't know," said the corpse at his feet.

Mavis looked up. Her breath hitched and she rubbed at the kink in her neck. "You were right. Tillie found Freddie."

"No I didn't," said Tillie.

The Hunger stirred awake. Mouths opened between its ribs and in the palms of its hands. Its fingers were as long as his forearms. Ivan's fists closed instinctively, and he put himself between it and the body he'd carried.

"He ate some of my spiders and came back to himself," said The Hunger. It spoke with many voices, and each of them sounded like his wife.

Ivan nodded and his eyebrows lifted at Mavis. "So killing Tillie wasn't the solution you thought it was."

"I don't know that she's capable of killing me," Tillie's voice echoed through all the mouths around him. Ivan sighed and shook his head. "Honey, pick a voice and stick with it. It's like you're speaking in a tunnel."

"Sorry," she answered from the body at his feet. "I'm going to..." The voice trailed away, and the beast fell apart.

Arms crawled around them, disjointed and jerking on their cut strings. They assembled near the torso at his feet, and Ivan's heart jumped into his throat. Spiders wove in and out of the bone until the many arms were joined. The consciousness carried between all her spiders were inextricably mixed, and there would be no discerning Hunger from his wife.

The body slowly stood up and steadied itself against a tree. Ivan offered his arm, watching her face as the spiders adjusted it minutely from behind the mask. The mask twitched and jumped, roiling with movement until it suddenly settled, and then Tillie smiled softly at him and took his arm.

"Are you okay?" she asked with her voice, with her expressions, with her love.

He let out the breath he'd been holding and pulled her into a hug. "It's still you."

She nodded. "It was always me. I'll try to keep it to one body. At least, one for now."

Ivan's face reddened as the force of a thousand pinprick eyes zeroed on him. "Honey, I think," he bit his lip and tried to speak delicately.

"I think there's got to be a serious ecological impact from eating an entire forest's fauna… It's really going to set us back on our climate pledge for the year."

"I know. I'm sorry. I'm a fucking disaster."

The boy stirred in Mavis's arms. He was beautiful: hair in a halo of dark curls, warm brown skin, long eyelashes. Feathers crowned his forehead, and his fingers were tipped in talons.

Tillie ducked behind Ivan's shoulder, multiple hands over her bashful face as she apologized for swearing around little Freddie.

Mavis's piercing eyes bore into her. "I don't think the fuck word is the worst thing he's experienced today."

Freddie's small hands grew into talons as they wrapped tight around Mavis's fingers, but the boy stayed mostly human as his eyes flicked over Tillie and Ivan.

Tillie crunched a five fingered hand in a friendly wave from around Ivan's shoulder. "Hi, Freddie. I'm your auntie."

Freddie stared with the same hard eyes as his mother. "Yes."

Mavis hugged him close. "He hasn't… I haven't heard his voice in months."

"You should have called sooner," said Ivan.

Mavis ducked her nose into Freddie's downy hair and blinked at persistent tears, but she did not speak.

"We're family," Ivan added, gently chiding. "We could have helped."

"She didn't know," said Tillie, softly, with a boney hand on his arm. Did not know they could have helped, or did not know that they were family; the words were applicable to both.

"You don't need to make excuses for her, Tillie. She tried to kill you."

Tillie shrugged. "I was going to eat her."

"Eat her," echoed Freddie. He plucked another spider from the ground and crunched it between blunt teeth.

"Does that hurt?" asked Ivan.

Tillie shook her head. "It feels odd, but it doesn't hurt. More like… like I forgot something, but I don't know what it was, and I can't remember if it was important or not."

Mavis brushed Freddie's feathers and smoothed his hair. "You're a bridge. There's enough human spirit in the spiders to satisfy him. When Mackenzie died, he thought his sacrifice could be enough to sustain him, but it lost its potency. We had to use more and more. What he thought could give us a lifetime only lasted a year."

Ivan rose up on his toes, grinning in spite of Mavis's somber air. "I was right," he said softly. Mavis glared at him, but he was undeterred. "The solution was buried in your partial success; you just needed a source of spirit that wouldn't lose its potency—" he cut himself off to look sharply at Tillie. "He'll need more." His eyes narrowed and he took her hand. "I don't want you losing memories for her." He jerked his head at Mavis.

"I can choose." Tillie sighed. "I don't need the small things. The color of the leaves on the witch hazel on March twenty-first three years ago sort of things." She shrugged. "I shouldn't have held onto all that, anyway. It got a little," she looked up at the massive construct of bone and web, "unwieldy." She breathed out a thin sigh and tilted her head toward the boy. "And it would be for him."

Mavis's dark eyes shifted between Ivan and Tillie. Her grip was tight around her son. She still managed to look prideful while sitting in the dirt. "I hate to ask anything of you," she started, slowly, as though the words had to be pried from her teeth.

"You don't have to ask," said Tillie. She sent more of herself crawling toward the boy in offering. He watched with mild curiosity, but made no move to strike them. The feathers had smoothed away to hair, and only his blackened nails and dark eyes carried hints of his affliction.

"Do you need a place to stay?" asked Ivan.

Mavis nodded, and her tears fell onto Freddie's hair.

"Your legs must be tired," said Tillie to Ivan. "I could carry us home, if you don't mind a ride inside The Hunger."

Ivan sighed and shrugged and went into the carriage of rib-bone and spidersilk. "I think we need a real movie day, honey. This has been a lot."

Tillie marched in after him. "Two movies," she agreed. "Maybe a whole day of movies. And I want to make some models for the train set while we watch them." She could uncover her legs from their place in the attic and see about finding a place for them. "There's a toy shop that I've been wanting to build."

Ivan perked at that and steepled his fingers in delight. "I could put a tiny train set in the window of the toy shop."

"I can paint it to match our own set!"

"Toy shop," Freddie repeated with reverence. His mother held him tighter and carried him into the hunger.

"It feels unfair," said Mavis, and the spiders nearest her tensed. "I was so afraid of you, and you've just been painting and building trains."

Tillie shrugged, then left her humanoid body to spin the construct of The Hunger to life. Mouths opened in the walls and under their feet. "I was also eating an entire forest, so..." The mouths hemmed and hawed in unison; a cacophony of indecision, until the one nearest Mavis found her words. "It's not like your fear was misplaced."

Ivan stared as the body rose and began to lumber its way through the forest. One of his hands was placed on the shoulder of Tillie's vacant human body as if steadying her on a shaky tram. His other was pressed deep into the web that caged them in, his fingers wrapped tight around bone.

"Sorry, honey," she whispered through a mouth that opened near his shoulder.

He leaned toward it and brushed his shoulder affectionately at the silk and bone surrounding him. "I was just admiring your pulley system for the limbs. There's a lot of engineering you put into these bodies, Tills."

"You're taking this all so well."

He shrugged. "I meant what I said." He kissed the wall of silk. "The only thing that scares me is losing you."

Mavis looked pointedly away, and hugged Freddie tight again.

A voice rumbled near her. "You're pretty with the gray hair, Mavis. Very distinguished."

"Really?" Mavis blushed and looked away, but she was surrounded by eyes. "You..." she gaped as she searched for words. Laughter broke out across the mouths that surrounded them.

"You don't have to say anything. I know what I look like."

"I bought all your books," Mavis said in a rush.

"What?"

She looked down at Freddie's feathery hair and combed it with her fingers to avoid Tillie's eyes. "All the books you illustrated. The magazines. Everything in print, and I printed a few of the online things, too."

Tillie pulled the bones closer around them; a phantom hug with a hundred thousand legs. "I missed you, too, Mavis. Stay with us for a little while. I want to get to know my nephew."

Mavis pressed her hand to the silk and brushed the spiders underneath. "I might need to stay indefinitely. I don't know if I can keep him human without you."

Ivan nodded. "Then stay."

All her mouths echoed his words, *stay stay stay*.

And they did.

Epilogue

The Woman Who Was Made Of One Hundred Thousand Spiders

The woman, the construct, the collective Tillie Wright was in the garden. The fence was high, the flowers higher, and a thick tangle of wisteria closed the sky above in a profusion of purple blossoms. Tillie's body wore long skirts to cover the many legs that held her torso aloft as she chose a chair beneath the wisteria. Many of her selves were crawling freely through the grass. Some were tending the new insect boxes. Some were monitoring the soil. Most were simply relaxing, because her friend had come to chat, and her sister was close by, and her nephew was playing dress up with the neighbor girl and screeching his little bird laugh while she painted his nails blue.

Ivan sat a tray of coffee on the garden table and leaned down to kiss Tillie's head. She wore her original skull with blue glass eyes fit neatly within the sockets, and she'd adopted the dead man's rib cage. She'd wrapped her original one in wads of paper and packed it in a wooden crate to go home with Leilani, who was explaining what her partner's work might entail.

"She can probably get it back to you within the week, if you need it," said Leilani.

"I don't want to rush her," said Tillie.

Ivan's hand squeezed around her shoulder. "You'll miss it, though," he added, softly, and he was right. She loved her first bones best, and her soul felt comfort when they were near. Ivan had helped her pull her legs out of storage when he picked a new model for the train set. The legs were useful, but the bones of the feet were fragile, and she was in the process of articulating the toes into sconces for the den where they could hold a glass shade and cast the room in a warm green glow.

"Bree was already hoping to meet you before the retreat. Now that she gets to fix your bones, she'll probably dive into the job the second I get home." Leilani laughed. "If you make her wait more than a week, she's going to explode."

"She wants to meet me?"

Leilani smiled. "I talk about you!" She said it with such ease, as if it should be obvious.

Ivan laughed and knocked his hip against Tillie's shoulder. "She's a fan of you, too," he said to Leilani, then wandered off to check on the kids.

Leilani raised her glass toward the neighbor girl, Ava. "Can she see it?" she whispered. Tillie was unsure what she meant. There were many things to see. The extra legs, the spiders all around them, the feathers that poked through Freddie's hair.

"No," said Mavis, who appeared like a shadow from behind them. "Tillie's glamour is..." she chewed over her words and finally settled on "Robust," with a tight smile. "The only reason you can see it is because you caught her in a moment of weakness."

"I'm not a witch, Mavis. I didn't set up any glamour." Mavis had one she'd stitched into her skin when she was twenty-three. Not for prettiness, that was something Mavis had naturally. Always had, with her hawk-like eyes and sharp nose. She had made it for power, so that no one would ever look at the five-foot nothing woman and see someone small.

Even without the yellow scales stitched into her skin, it seemed the glamour held. Or perhaps Mavis had adopted it into herself long before she lost her magic and made it true.

Mavis clicked her tongue against her teeth. "What do you think this is?" She waved her hand at Tillie's face. "Magic is more about the work than the specific ritual. And this is," her eyebrow raised at the concert of spiders that worked to turn Tillie's head, to make her expressions, to speak and laugh and paint and love with a singular soul. "This is a lot of work, and a lot of ritual."

"I could have left the house a long time ago," whispered Tillie. She had spent ten years perfecting her human mask, creating the artist's body, and only trusted it to leave the house for a week. "I wish I'd known."

A grimace flashed across Mavis's face and disappeared before it could upset the placid calm she always wore. "I should have helped you... I'm sorry."

Tillie put on a brave face. "You didn't know either. There's no sense in dwelling in should-haves." She reached for Mavis's hand, and a hundred thousand hearts fluttered as Mavis reached back and wrapped her fingers around Tillie's silken palm. "I'm glad you're here now."

Mavis's fingers flexed around her glass of water and she nodded curtly to her son playing happily in the yard. "I'm glad too." Her voice cracked over the words and she looked away. But Tillie had eyes everywhere in the yard, and there was a sheen of tears in Mavis's eyes.

"Can I hug you?" asked Tillie. She'd spent the week in a delicate dance around Mavis and Freddie. There was so much to do, to build the spare room into a home, to make the living room fun and fit for a four-year-old. It was easy to be busy, to give Mavis space, to talk around the hole that she left and the ache of the years between them. She didn't know if she ever could talk about it.

So they talked about Freddie. And art. And Mackenzie, when Mavis felt strong enough to share what she missed about him.

"It's okay to say no. I've only hugged two people since I died and if you're not comfortable—"

Mavis wrapped her arms tight around Tillie's shoulder and exhaled into her hair. "Thank you." Tears fell into the silk and Mavis hurriedly brushed them away, but Tillie squeezed her arms to make her stop.

"It's alright. I'm not as fragile as I look."

"Mom is sad." Freddie stood at the edge of the shaded space where his mom and auntie and auntie's friend were sitting. When viewed from all her eyes, he was a dazzling kaleidoscope of shadow and light, feathers and hair, soft skin and scale and hard black nails that came to points. And when she focused, and brought her vision back to the favored eye that sat on her left shoulder, tucked into the forest green scarf, he was still dazzling. A nephew. An extension of her family, long after the point when she should have ever known him.

"Not sad, honey," said Mavis, wiping a tear from her eye. "Sometimes when mommy is very happy, the feelings come out like tears."

Freddie ran into the shaded place and dug his little talons into Tillie's skirt and skin as he scrabbled onto her lap. "Auntie happy, too?"

Tillie nodded and squeezed him to her chest. "So happy."

Ivan coughed politely somewhere over her shoulder. Tillie turned her head, but he wasn't in the yard. A brief confluence between all of her bodies alerted her to where he stood in the studio. Where she'd tucked her artist's body away to finish an illustration while the rest of her enjoyed the company of her friends. She turned to him and wheeled her chair back from the work she'd been buried in, her head sheepishly bowed. She suppressed the urge to swipe a brush of pink across her mask to mimic the blush she felt across her selves.

"Sorry."

"I thought you were keeping it to one body."

"I should," she said quickly. The body outside ran its fingers through Freddie's feathery hair. It smiled at Leilani. It asked what she was working on next, now that the retreat was done. It carried on with ease, just as this plastic body lived contentedly within the studio, painting the memory of waves.

Water was easier to love when it was safely tucked within memory.

"I'm not mad," said Ivan. He moved a stack of paper off of a folding chair and pulled it to sit across from her desk.

She sat higher than him on the wheelchair, and she felt a little sheepish over that, too. Everything had felt a little off in the week since he'd discovered The Hunger. Like none of her bodies fit the same as before, and everything in her house had been moved an inch to the left.

"But I promised—" she started, and he stopped her.

"You didn't. You didn't promise one body, and I don't think I'd like that, anyway." He found one of her biggest spiders crawling up the wall, where it was climbing to re-stick some tape that had lost its tack. He let it crawl into his hand and brought it down to his lap, where he could stroke a single finger over its head. "One body can't hold my hand. Or give me a hug." He kissed the spider on its thorax and set it down on her desk. It crawled across and placed itself on her lap, and she curled her human fingers around it. Holding herself as she wondered what to say.

"You don't have to pretend to be human."

"I do." So much of the world was beyond her reach. Pretending brought close. Enough to almost touch.

"Not with me." He reached for her, but she could not tell if he was reaching for the plastic hand or for the spider it was curled around. She gave him both, and he entwined their fingers as his thumb touched the spider's claw. "I know that it feels like everything is different now, but it's better. To me, it's better."

She shook her head. She'd been so frazzled through the week as she helped her sister and nephew settle. And while she had countless spiders to keep him fed, it was a struggle to sort the memories she was willing to give.

"What if I forget the parts of me that remember being human?" The spiders in her lungs froze. She did not mean to speak that part out loud. His eyebrows raised, and she whispered, "What if I become something that wasn't her?"

"Do you think I remember exactly what I was like ten years ago?"

"That's different."

"It isn't. I didn't know what I'd be now. I don't know what I'll be in another ten. But I'm not afraid of the future so long as we're together."

"God, you're perfect." She tried to sigh and it turned into a laugh.

He chuckled and pulled her arm toward him, not even pausing when it came loose in his hand. He set it on the desk and leaned across to brush his nose across her cheek, nuzzle in and kiss her mask beneath the empty eyes. She closed the lids and returned his kiss, pressing as hard as she dared, and some of the cobweb skin of her lips came away on his stubble.

No matter. A simple repair.

He rubbed it away and presented it back to her with the solemnity of a wedding ring and smiled when she laughed at his antics.

"You're perfect," he accused, then sat back down on the folding chair. "Tell me what you're painting."

She drew in a breath and alighted on the opportunity to speak of how light played with the waves on the beach, how she discovered what to love about the water and how she wanted to depict it in paint.

He looked over her shoulder with his hand resting on her arm. A spider brushed its mouth against his fingertip and savored the imperceptible lift of oil and skin, and it tasted just like love.

Acknowledgements

This is a book about the need for connection in spite of one's self-imposed hermitage, and in keeping with that theme, I have a community to thank for the creation of this novella. My incredible editor Abby Muller's careful eye and brilliant understanding of the story made this book far better than I could have managed on my own, and I will be forever grateful for her involvement.

My writing group: Katrina, Sam, and Michael. Thank you for helping me float through the long fallow periods of my writing life, and for giving me space to revisit a story when it is time for it. Sam is also my audio narrator, and the desire to hear their monster voice for The Hunger played a significant role in my desire to see this work finished.

To Kij and Barbara, my instructors at Novel Architects. I am sorry to inform you that I finished the first draft of this when I should have been working on something more novel shaped. However, the lessons I learned there did allow me to reach an ending, even if this book falls about 40k short of a full novel.

To the many friends I've made in my writing life; I could not ask for a better and more welcoming community than the people who write spec-fic, and although I am often at the edges, wondering how to break the ice, if we've ever talked shop at cons or online, or somewhere else in the margins, please know that you are dear to me.

And, although he does not know me, I am thankful to Keven Brockmeier for choosing to publish the first story featuring my spider woman all the way back in 2014. Its inclusion in The Iowa Review allowed me to weather multiple depressive periods where I managed to convince myself I'd lost the ability to write.

My family, my mom and dad and brother who encourage my writing, who ask me what I'm working on, and are excited about the work even when it gets weird. Thank you.

My kids, Eleanor and Henry, whose presence in my life have changed me in mysterious and irrevocable ways. I had been trying to write a sequel to Tillie's story for ten years, but until I had you, I could not see the shape of it. I love you both.

And of course, my husband, Erik Hosa. Without you, this would not have been a love story. Without you, it could not have been written at all. Thank you for believing in me far better than I could.

ABOUT THE AUTHOR

Megan Lee Bees is an author and illustrator from Tacoma, Washington, where she lives with her husband, her twin children, and a formally feral cat. She has published short fiction in a variety of markets, including The Iowa Review, Cast of Wonders, and Underland Arcana's Cozy Cosmic anthologies.

find more at www.meganleebees.com

www.ingramcontent.com/pod-product-compliance
Lightning Source LLC
LaVergne TN
LVHW020443070526
838199LV00063B/4834